Just Like You

Just Like You

Nichola D. Gutgold

Mt. Nittany Press
Lemont

© 2018 by Nichola D. Gutgold
Cover art by Rachel C. Ferguson
Printed in the United States of America

All rights reserved. This publication is protected by Copyright, and permission should be obtained from the publisher prior to any prohibited reproduction, storage in a retrieval system, or transmission in any form or by any means, electronic, mechanical, photocopying, recording, or likewise.

Published by Mt. Nittany Press, an imprint of Eifrig Publishing,
PO Box 66, Lemont, PA 16851.
Knobelsdorffstr. 44, 14059 Berlin, Germany

For information regarding permission, write to:
Rights and Permissions Department,
Eifrig Publishing,
PO Box 66, Lemont, PA 16851, USA.
permissions@eifrigpublishing.com, 888-340-6543.

Library of Congress Cataloging-in-Publication Data

Gutgold, Nichola D., Just Like You

p. cm.

Paperback: ISBN 978-1-63233-180-9
Hardcover: ISBN 978-1-63233-181-6
eBook: ISBN 978-1-63233-182-3

I. Gutgold, Nichola D., II. Title.

22 21 20 19 2018
5 4 3 2 1

Printed on acid-free paper. ∞

For my parents Julia and Nicholas DelBalso,
who are always with me.
N.D.G.

Chapter 1

Denise was in a tailspin all day. She forgot to pick up Renee, their youngest child, from school to take her to dance class. Then Clark, their 14-year-old, didn't come home after school, and she forgot to check on him. At least the two older Ferraro children were at college, and the helpful neighbors in their close-knit community readily stepped in with carpools and an occasional meal if they needed help. Without medication to keep her mood swings at bay, Denise struggled, and it would not be the first time child services stepped in. The Ferraro children were forced to grow up fast. By the time Casimer returned home, exhausted after a long day running his IT company, his patience was thin.

He asked Denise, "Did you take your medicine?"

Denise didn't answer, she just laughed.

Nothing is funny about this.

At 45 Casimir was still a head-turner. Tall and as thin as he was in high school, his thick black hair was lustrous and meticulously styled. A sharp dresser, he resembled his Sicilian father, although his mother's family, from Poland, provided his name. He was Cas to everyone. He had built a successful business. He was a well-known community leader.

Still in her slept-in yoga pants and rumpled tee shirt, Denise had the TV on in the master bedroom, one eye on *The Real Housewives of New York* and another on Penelope, the family cat on the windowsill. She was unsteady on her feet, laughing in a drunken fog, when Cas insisted that she take her medication. Denise washed the pills down with another glass of Riesling, and moved to the window for fresh air.

Since Cas had not gotten around to installing the screens on the windows, her slight frame fit easily through the opening.

Penelope let out a plaintive meow as Denise fell two stories onto the driveway below.

Cas ran downstairs, felt no pulse, and frantically called 911, as adrenaline coursed through him. Yet part of him felt deeply relieved that his wife of more than two decades was gone.

By this time, swarms of nosy neighbors from the cul-de-sac gathered. When the police arrived Cas was crying inconsolably.

Five Years Later
Chapter 2

Stacey reminded Zach about his History Day Project spread out on the floor of the dining room and told Chloe to pack her cheerleading clothes for practice after school. She was warming up her SUV in the garage when Grant poured her a second cup of coffee for the road and gave her a quick kiss. The commute to the kids' schools and her bridal salon, Golden Day Bridals, was more than thirty minutes from their sprawling country home, and on most days Stacey wished they had bought a place closer to everything.

Even a cookie cutter two-story colonial would be better than the inconvenience of this monstrosity.

It was big with an extra sun room and sturdy, energy-saving 2x6 construction, as Grant liked to remind her, but that was a cold comfort to Stacey, who spent most of the day strapped in the driver's seat of her "mom-mobile" chauffeuring Chloe and Zach around. She no sooner came home and prepared a quick dinner, when it was time to turn around for dance, cheerleading, scouts, or some other bit of must-do enrichment.

Grant always made the coffee, great coffee at that. He daydreamed of one day opening a gourmet coffee roasting cafe, but for now he was consumed with his work as an engineer for an international chemical company, and his other job—staying up in the grill of everyone in the house, even house guests, about turning off lights and keeping the heat and air conditioning low. Grant was fully committed to saving money, and though not yet born when Jimmy Carter served as president, he lived each day as a devotee to the energy crisis. A middle school lesson turned lifelong philosophy, lower energy costs mattered more than almost anything else, and he tuned out of the day-to-day particulars of his family's lives. Somehow this became Stacey's job.

With support from Grant's parents only during the part of the year they were not in Florida, Stacey was forced into Wonder Woman role—mom, business owner, volunteer. And most people would tell you that Stacey Falesh-Gutton *was* Wonder Woman. A petite powerhouse, she kept herself, and her house, humming. She worked out to a "walk-at-home video" every morning before she headed into the shower, and she assiduously watched her weight. A vegetarian since her middle school days, she was a foodie, but she focused on calorie control and whole foods, and it was working.

She wasn't one of the super-skinny moms who spent their days at the gym, but she was well proportioned, and her hair was always meticulously styled, her blond highlights framing her girlish face, dominated by huge blue eyes. As a bridal salon owner, she knew that customers were judging her on her appearance and sense of style, so she dressed well in sleek dresses and boots. She always looked pulled together, and she didn't spend a fortune on it either. She had style savvy and could create a striking look with the right scarf or a pretty statement necklace. Her customers seemed impressed. It was likely the busiest time of her life, and yet, to the outside world, Stacey appeared to be holding it together with finesse.

She often caught herself dreaming of more sleep, and

was even too exhausted lately to glance at the newspaper. She missed her favorite section, the obituaries. Odd to some perhaps, Stacey enjoyed reading about the dead and pondering the age-old question: *what makes a good life*? Both of her parents died before they were 70, and it made her more than a bit obsessed with mortality. She knew, more keenly than most her age, that life has an ever-pending expiration date.

Therefore, keep watch. We know not the day nor the hour.

It saddened her that neither her mom or dad had the joy of knowing Chloe and Zach, and perhaps selfishly, she knew that she would have felt so much less stressed to have her parents in their lives. She felt envy when one of her friends spoke of their mothers coming to help them bake cookies for Christmas, or offering to help them shop for back-to-school clothes with their kids. Even in mid-life, she longed for the unconditional support of parental love. Just a gold star here or there, a "good job, kiddo," or a "we're proud of you," once in a while, would have made all the difference. *Someone on her side.*

Every minute of every day, even more than a decade after their deaths, Stacey missed her parents, and the support and love that they could offer. This longing for them was simply a part of her, an appendage as much as her constantly lit-up cell phone. All things considered, she really couldn't complain about too much, and above all, she was not a complainer. She knew people who seemed to love nothing more than a good whining session, and she did not want to ever turn into a middle-aged disappointed person. She made a point to distance herself from people like that, and she hired preternaturally cheerful people for the salon too. Who wants to buy a wedding dress from a grouch?

She and Grant had built a good life, and they both worked hard. Grant was kind in small ways, like bringing her a bundle of flowers each week, and trying to listen when she felt upset about something at work. He did seem to grasp that she really missed her parents, and overall, he wanted to be understanding and a good husband. He had not become wicked in the way middle-aged men sometimes do with a roving eye, seemingly mad at the world for what they had failed to become, or disappointed that their wives were not the carefree girls they had married. Grant was sweet, decent, and kind. He admired, if not worshipped Stacey, knowing deep in his heart that she was exceptional in many ways. He was thrifty to the point of discomfort, and often too preoccupied with his own work responsibilities to be the sympathetic friend that Stacey really needed. But she loved him. She wished that he looked at her adoringly when she entered a room, or sang her praises, especially in the absence of her parents, but whose marriage is just how they wished it to be? Grant was a good person, and with each passing year she was more and more proud of the life they had built together.

At least we're not divorced.

Not quite five foot eight, Grant hit the gym every day, didn't smoke and rarely drank. Dressed in his khaki pants and a navy blazer, he kissed Stacey lightly on the cheek and headed out for his work day.

"I may be late," he said, moving toward the door. "Corporate is coming all week and I'll probably have to do some lunches and dinners. I'll call you by six if I won't be home for dinner."

"Shouldn't you be wearing a tie?" Stacey asked, with her right eyebrow going up a bit higher than usual. "You know, for corporate," she added.

"Good call," he said, as he headed back upstairs to grab one.

It was true that Stacey was somewhat of a fashion police, especially with Grant, since it seemed that no one ever taught him basic dressing tips. He had come a long way since she met him: shaggy beard, wrinkled pants, too big dress shirts, but he could definitely step it up a notch. Once a year, he'd dash into the mall with a pile of coupons and come out with five ill-fitting, odd-colored dress shirts on sale from a discount store, and add them to his closet filled with clothing he hadn't worn in years. She tried to help him sort out his pants and shirts, making a pile for charity, only to find him adding the clothes from the "discarded" pile back to his closet when she wasn't looking. He hated to discard anything, even ripped or soiled clothes. He'd call them "painting clothes," but Stacey never saw him paint anything. Though she had bought him several expensive, custom-tailored sport coats, he never wore them. Instead he preferred the same worn-out, baggy navy blazer he owned since Zach's baptism. More than a dozen times he had to borrow a sport coat at restaurants that required one, simply because he didn't think to wear one.

Grant still dutifully packed his own lunch so that if the office wasn't heading out with the corporate folks for lunch, he could stay at his desk, working in solitude through the lunch hour. He preferred it that way. Once he did the math, and boasted that if he ate lunch at his desk instead of going out to a restaurant over the course of a thirty-year career, he'd save $80,000.

Even with Grant's lack of fashion sense, he and Stacey were a diminutively handsome couple, and, as he made his way out the door to slay the dragons at the chemical company, armed with his lunch and coffee cup, he gently touched Chloe's hair and mock-fist Zach's upper arm.

"Bye, dad," they sang in unison.

As Grant left, Stacey and the kids piled into her SUV, emblazoned with the Golden Day Bridal Salon logo in red and gold on the back and they headed in the opposite directions.

Chapter 3

Stacey dropped both kids off at school, and started toward her salon. As she drove up she could see the lights were already on. Golden Day Bridals grew from a modest shop in her basement, where a bride—usually a daughter of a friend—would order her dress from a catalog. Eventually it became a nationally recognized upscale bridal salon. Stacey even appeared on the national cable show *You've Got To Buy That Dress!* as a bridal styling expert, and her profile in the bridal industry was growing by the minutes.

She had a good team, and Nancy was not only a great employee, she was her good friend. It was a comforting to have such a warm friendship that she could multi-task with work. She didn't carve out time for "mom" fun. Between her business and Grant and the kids, she didn't keep a commitment to a monthly book club or Bunko night. She sometimes leaned on Nancy for support, and Nancy did the same.

Stacey had what her sister Teri liked to call "trouble in the Green Monster" department when it came to female friendships. Stacey would think that she had a friend, only to learn that she said something snarky behind her back, or undermined her in some way. Nancy and her husband had a good relationship, and though they would have liked to have kids, they married in their late thirties. When it didn't happen, they poured their love and attention into their dog and other people's kids. Zach and Chloe even called them aunt and uncle.

"There's fresh coffee in the back," is how she greeted Stacey, and "Your hair looks good, and oh, the mail from the weekend is back there too. Something from Bishop Frances High School even!"

That was a name Stacey hadn't heard in years. Bishop Frances High School: her high school. Just hearing the name had transported her back to the day she pleaded with her parents to attend the Catholic high school across town after participating in a softball league and meeting some girls the summer before her ninth grade year. It was not even her parish high school, but her mom said she could go, as long as the diocese approved it. And like most of the things she wanted to do, her mom was supportive in every way. Stacey reflected back on her mom's positive influence in her life on a daily basis all these years later.

Mom just made things happen for me. That high school changed my life.

Stacey and her sisters were not spoiled growing up, far from it, but their mom and dad wanted them to follow their passions and tried to help them any way that they could. Stacey was the same way with Chloe and Zach: Space Camp, Seaworld Camp, private schools. Nothing was too much. She was stereotypical in her first-generation striving to give the kids good lives. She did whatever it took to make the extra money that all the enrichment required, taking on consulting assignments, writing a blog on fashion for a local style magazine, and even teaching a course on event planning at a local community college. Sometimes Stacey's generosity with Chloe and Zach caused problems with Grant because he was raised more hardscrabble. Though his parents both had educations beyond high school, they didn't pay for or even help him or his brother to go to college, making both of their lives more difficult.

It wasn't as though they outright refused, per se, but they didn't save much money, and they didn't show much enthusiasm or interest in helping either of them truly consider options upon high school graduation. It was the most perplexing thing to Stacey, and she could see signs of that same antipathy toward the children in Grant. As much as she searched the depths of her compassion, she just could not understand it. Grant had to work a full time job while he went to college part time, and it had made him especially thrifty and reluctant to give the kids things he never got. "Stop giving them so much," he would say to Stacey, but she wanted to. She wanted them to have the same opportunities she had.

If that's my crime, giving my kids too many opportunities, then lock me up!

She experienced first hand the benefits of supportive, generous parents.

The kids who went to Bishop Frances were more like her. Their parents provided them with opportunities, and because of it, their futures were brighter. Almost all the kids at her high school, even the ones who probably should not have gone, went to college or a trade school. And the atmosphere at Bishop Frances was just nicer than the public school-- there were mother-daughter teas, father-daughter dances, formal dress dances, and plays. It instilled in Stacey that these little things, these social moments, made life more beautiful and memorable and that manners matter. If the principal knew of one student making another student feel badly, that kid was in his office, and the punishment was severe. In junior year the whole school participated in a day of kindness in honor of a boy who died of cancer. It was a world that Stacey never saw before she went there, and she loved it. And what she loved most was the yearly Mother's Club Fashion Show. It's where her interest in formal attire started. Her mother, seeing her natural talent and enthusiasm, urged her to follow her passion and open a bridal salon. Right after graduating college, Stacey worked for a large, well-known bridal shop in Philadelphia, and then after her mom died, she started her own salon in honor of her mom with the modest inheritance she received. Every day she went to Golden Day Bridals, she felt she was honoring her mom. Her mom was from such difficult, modest financial circumstances, that she never even had a wedding dress when she got married. That's the kind of people Stacey came from. Big hearted people who wanted more for their children, not less. It was a good feeling, and it lessened the heartbreak she endured when her parents died.

She always called Golden Day a "mission driven dream," and her staff the "dream team." She was a good boss, and tried to make work as fun and meaningful as possible. There may have been drama between the moms and daughters over what dress was best, but the staff of Golden Day Bridals was drama-free. They got along, and knew that they were doing more than selling bridal dresses. They were making one of the most important days in a family's life more beautiful. The jingle for the salon echoed that sentiment, and it blared throughout the store and over the radio and television airwaves. In an upbeat staccato the woman's voice boomed: "We make your dreams come true at Golden Day Bridal Salon where all that glitters is Golden. Golden Day Bridals—let us make *your* dreams come true!"

Stacey opened the Bishop Frances envelope. The school had closed more than five years ago because of budget cutbacks. Like so many ethnic churches, Catholic schools kept shrinking in numbers, but the planning committee for the reunion still used the familiar block lettered logo on the mailing, and she could see that Mary Ann Redds was the committee chairperson. Not surprising. Mary Ann and Stacey had been friends, and even went to Philadelphia to see a Rick Summerville concert together their senior year. Stacey remembers being so impressed that even though they were just high schoolers, Mary Ann drove to Philadelphia for the concert and even planned the whole rest of the evening, making sure that they took in some Philadelphia landmarks. She was an events planner in the making, and Stacey pictured the new, grown-up boots she wore to the big city concert: low white cowboy boots with long fringe around the top. More than one man gave her a lusty double-take as they made their way from Mary Ann's mom's station wagon to the auditorium. Not yet seventeen, Stacey had the look of a twenty-year-old woman, full of wide-eyed innocence and wonder in her tight dark denim designer jeans and white rabbit fur coat. She begged her mom for that coat, and remembers her Aunt Teresa giving her mother ten dollars towards the adorable, fluffy coat for her sweet sixteen. Mary Ann Redds was a leader then and now, and obviously Stacey's penchant for style was taking shape all those years ago. So much of who we are is settled for us early in life. *We are who we are.*

"*Remember, We're Vikings Forever! Reunion Weekend — Don't Miss It!*" blared across the front of the invitation, but Stacey didn't give it much thought, tossing it onto a stack of mounting invitations and notices.

Nice of Mary Ann to do all the planning, but actually getting alumni to be there? How will that even happen? Aren't most of us knee-deep in child rearing and career obligations? Maybe just the locals will show.

In her mind, there were just too many day-to-day demands to spend time reminiscing about high school. Hard to believe more than twenty years passed. She had so many good memories about Bishop Frances, and though she wasn't a philosopher, she knew one thing for sure: life is short. She rifled through a few more invitations. The kids' school was having a parent "coffee and conversation" night, and Stacey cared about keeping up with the school news, but felt ambivalence about actually attending. The last one turned into a gossip session among the other parents, and it made Stacey uncomfortable.

Stacey poured herself another cup of coffee and headed to the front of the store as Lisa and Martin, two other Golden Day employees, were coming in. It was a full day of appointments—even a media interview with the local newspaper on emerging bridal trends—and Stacey needed all hands on deck to get it done. She was happy to steal away for a quick lunch of vegetable soup and crackers at her desk. Grant encouraged her to make a batch of vegetable soup every Sunday night, and he packed his lunch for the week with it, marveling at how a whole crock pot of vegetable soup came out to only five dollars. Stacey spread the Dawn Chronicle out and pored over the obituaries as usual. She often got lost in the details of the deceased lives. Though she didn't know any of them, she pondered what each person must have really been like simply by reading the entries submitted by grieving loved ones.

How is a whole life distilled in 200 words? And why did newspapers charge so much money for obituaries?

For a long time she thought about Corinne Renee Blue. Mother of Derek and Cindy. Worked thirty years as a staff assistant at the local Penn State campus. Valiantly fought two battles against breast cancer. Loved fly fishing and watching the Eagles with her husband of thirty years, Alan. Will be missed and remembered for her devotion to her family.

Wow. So sad. Only sixty two.

Stacey moved onto the obituary of a man who was ninety-six. He was survived by sixteen grandchildren.

Lots of typos in his obituary that seemed to be hastily written, as if they family wasn't expecting it. At ninety-six, how can the family not be expecting it? Or maybe they were just lousy writers. Who was it that said people either die too early or too late?

Stacey was startled back to reality, even jumping a little in her chair, when Nancy called out to tell her that the sales rep from Nera Savoy was on the phone, confirming she would join the team with the new Spring Look Book for the upcoming meeting in Philadelphia. Getting lost in the obituary section was the closest thing Stacey had to a flow state. *Who needs yoga and meditation when you have dead people?*

"Pick up your extension, Stacey, Courtney Phillips is on the line," Nancy yelled back. *Lunchtime is over. Note to self: need an upgraded phone system. Yelling to the back of my office is not very classy for an up and coming bridal empire.*

When the hectic work week ended it wasn't even time for a day off. Instead, the entire Golden Day Bridal team would be headed to Philadelphia for their annual three-day strategic planning retreat. It was a busy week and weekend ahead for Stacey and the Golden Day dream team. Time to brew another pot of coffee.

Chapter 4

When Stacey began holding retreats a few years back at the luxurious Ritz-Carlton in Philadelphia, Grant warned her that it was too extravagant, but Stacey felt otherwise.

"Treat others as you wish to be treated, and if you're the boss, you will get it back in performance and loyalty," she assured him. She told Grant he ought to try it. He complained that the money she laid out for the Ritz-Carlton weekend could be going to the kids' college funds, but she disagreed wholeheartedly. Spending out is what she called it, but Grant was always so thrifty with everything. When she asked for a luxury handbag for her birthday, he bought one from a resale website. He was forever lowering the heat in the house in the winter, and shutting off the air conditioning in the summer. There were just a few days all year that the house actually felt comfortable, just as summer ended and before the cold days of winter started. She learned to cope, but his thriftiness caused a lot of irritation over the years, and very little cost savings as she could see it.

On Saturday, after the last fitting at Golden Day, Stacey, Lisa, Nancy and Martin all piled into Stacey's SUV for the one hour trip to Philadelphia. Closing the store on Monday and paying for the weekend stay at the Ritz would be pricey, but Stacey knew it would yield a great return on investment. The staff looked forward to the retreat, and this year Stacey added spa services for each of them to show her appreciation. It had been a record year. The exposure from *You've Got To Buy That Dress!* was making Stacey, and Golden Day famous. Eager mothers and daughters were driving right past long established wedding dress stores in upscale areas of Philadelphia and New Jersey for a chance to be consulted by Stacey and her staff. And the two most popular bridal salons for years in the Lehigh Valley closed in the past couple years. Stacey was a natural on camera. She was photogenic, funny, and always kind, but direct about what looked best on a bride. It was her winning ways that were gaining a following for Golden Day. She hired an intern, Meg, from Cedar Point College to handle social media, and if the response on social media continued, she told her that a full time position would be created once she graduated. She needed someone to field calls from the press, generate new publicity, organize branding efforts, and Meg was enthusiastic and competent.

Martin offered to drive to Philadelphia, and Stacey gladly accepted. When they pulled onto the Avenue of the Arts, The Ritz-Carlton was aglow for the evening. "Nothing for tonight, team, I'm beat," Stacey said. "But look over the weekend's agenda, and come to my room in the morning, the Presidential Suite, at eight ready to roll up your sleeves and get to work!" They were all happy to retire to their rooms. Passing the grand marble staircase, flanked by enormous orchid filled urns, they said their good nights and retreated to their luxurious rooms.

Stacey booked superior rooms for each of them. They would be pleased to see that they had a gorgeous view of the city and a generously sized work space. Stacey even sent up small welcome baskets for each of them, noting their favorite wine, cheese and chocolate preferences. For herself, The Presidential Suite. Why not? She rationalized that the living-room sized workspace would be nice for all of them to conduct a brainstorming session the following morning. She was impressed by all the details: the towel warmer, the fully stocked mini fridge, spa robe, and even a welcome basket she didn't order. They thought of everything here. She opened the little note inside the envelope on the basket of fruit and champagne. "Dear Ms. Falesh-Gutton, Welcome Back to the Ritz-Carlton. Enjoy your Stay. With our Compliments, Reginald Richards and staff." One thing Stacey knew for sure was that Grant would never spring for this. It always brought her down when they traveled, and he'd complain about the menu prices. She would be all keyed up for the trip and the chance to try a new restaurant, and Grant would open the menu and say, "$12.00 for a glass of Prosecco. What a rip-off!" She always felt that if you are going to take a vacation or go out to dinner, enjoy it, or just stay home. At least now she could splurge. Golden Day Bridals was her business, it was doing better than ever, and she would run it the way she wanted.

Bring on the twelve dollar Prosecco and whatever else you have, Philadelphia!

Her first instinct was to crawl under the down comforter and put on her favorite murder mystery show, *Die Time*, when she realized that she was not only tired, she was starving. She worked right through dinner, never stopped for a break, and now it was going on nine. She could feel her stomach begging for food, and she thought it wiser to eat something healthy than raid the mini-fridge. It was rare for Stacey to forget about eating, because as a foodie, she was always thinking about what she would have next. She thought to call room service and then realized it might be nice to people watch at the lobby bar and enjoy a relaxing, late dinner, alone with her thoughts and a rare moment to contemplate her life objectively. She grabbed her new(ish) Louis Vuitton bag from Grant, put her boots back on and headed downstairs.

There were about a dozen well-dressed patrons at the swank Lobby Bar when she arrived. She took a seat at the bar, and could see the dapper local Channel 10 meteorologist and his wife at a table nearby. She felt the eyes of a pretty young woman looking at her. This was becoming more common since she started appearing on TV. She could see the young woman whisper to her friend and then look over again. They got up and walked toward her. "Are you Stacey from *You've Got to Buy That Dress?*" one asked. She posed for a photo, signed their napkins and returned to her menu with a rush she got every time she was recognized in public. She had to pinch herself. The little, wide-eyed schoolgirl in her big sister's hand me downs turned napkin autographer. She chuckled to herself, and at the same time, felt so blessed for her success. She never took it for granted, and she always remembered where she came from.

Does being recognized in public make me successful?

As she looked up from the menu and surveyed the crowd at the bar she took in the well-heeled, polished scene. The menu was extensive for a bar menu, and she settled on a nice glass of Chardonnay, and a salad of heirloom tomatoes, beets and goat cheese. More than five years ago, she lost twenty-five pounds with Pounds Down, and she was doing a good job keeping her weight down. It was torture to lose the weight, and she hated every single photo she saw of herself when she was heavier, so she was determined not to gain her weight back. Within minutes her wine and salad arrived and she started eating slowing, relishing every bite, while enjoying the man at the piano, singing softly. She could feel her shoulders relaxing for the first time in a long time. Stacey Falesh-Gutton was still a beautiful woman, and with the increasing success of Golden Day Bridals, she was feeling like a highly successful one too. She closed her eyes as the singer crooned, "No New Year's Day to Celebrate, no chocolate cups, candy hearts to give away." A true romantic, she always loved this song from Stevie Wonder.

"Stacey, is that you?"

Her mouth went dry and she felt an old familiar pang in her stomach. She looked up, blinking her eyes and squinting, staring as if to examine something rare and strange, to be sure she was seeing what she was seeing. She could barely get the words out. "Cas? Oh, my goodness. It has been so long."

Chapter 5

Back home, Grant was managing just fine with the kids, especially since he brought in backup: his parents. It was late September. Betta (short for Elizabeth) and Isaac still had not left for winter at their Florida condo, so Grant asked them to stay the weekend and help him take care of Chloe and Grant so that he could get some work done. The kids were almost at the age that they didn't need any supervision, but Grant liked to stay close to his parents, and having them come over was a way to keep them actively involved in their lives. It was also his key to having time all to himself all weekend without cooking. Betta enjoyed cooking and took over the kitchen when she babysat. They sometimes seemed a little put out about babysitting, but they had a hard time coming up with an excuse, since they truly had nothing else to do, and they really loved their son.

Grant had a late dinner with corporate on Friday night, so "Granny" made dinner and played rounds of Uno with Zach. She and Zach shared a special bond. From the time he was a preemie, born six weeks early, Granny Betta marveled at his keen intelligence and loved his broad smile. And Zach adored his Granny, even calling her "Mom Two" when he was a little boy. Chloe was close to Granny and Pop-Pop, too, but in a different way. Being the only granddaughter, she had a place of honor in the family. They were good grandparents. Having both retired early, they filled their days with discount shopping and routine doctor visits. Neither was particularly demanding on Grant or his brother Garth's time. They showed up for holidays, pitched in to help with the grandchildren--there were five with Garth's three boys--and they played a nurturing role for the family. Betta read a lot, and clipped mounds of recipes from the magazines in the doctor's' offices. Though it was just the two of them, she stockpiled food in a large freezer so that she could prepare any favorite meal for anyone who came by.

They would leave in a couple of weeks for Vacation Village in Sun Beach, and their one-bedroom condo reserved for the 55+ set. At 70 and 65, they were among the youngest "snow birds," and they loved the warm weather and new bargain shopping to explore. Isaac seemed to be growing bored with it, but Betta loved it. She could swim every day in the large, heated pool, and she always made new friends each season.

Last week Stacey enthused that it was almost time to "go back to paradise," but Isaac grumbled, "The big thrill for everyone there is the 'Early Bird dinner!'"

Betta replied, "That's true, but I make you your 'Early Bird' dinner every night before you fall asleep on the couch by eight!"

They argued a lot, but Stacey could not tell if it was real or a performance. She often felt uncomfortable, but that was the Guttons, and there was nothing she could do about it. She came from a tranquil home where her parents almost never argued. They were deferential and soft spoken to each other. She remembers her father's conclusion at every homemade family meal: "Thank the good Lord for such a delicious meal, and thanks to Mom for making it."

Isaac was more likely to criticize Betta for making the wrong vegetable or not seasoning the main dish to his liking yet he never lifted a finger to assist. She dutifully served him breakfast, lunch and dinner, and complained about it to anyone who would listen.

Stacey missed her parents even more now that she had children of her own. To speak with her parents about her life would be so comforting. It was challenging to raise a family, and backup is always a comfort. Even a quick phone call at the end of the day would have been a Godsend. Sometimes, Stacey would just speak to the air, conversing with her parents as a way to feel close to them again. She'd say, "Chloe made the cheer team, Mom," or "Zach is on the honor roll, as usual."

When struggling with a decision to make, she'd do the same thing: "Should we let Chloe go to London with her 10th grade?" or "Is football too rough a sport for Zach?"

She wanted to have this kind of closeness with her in-laws, especially Betta, but when she did seek out her mother-in-law's advice, looking for sage guidance from someone who had been there, it often ended with Betta recounting how unfair it was when her children were growing up, how she never had it easy, that Isaac was no help, lacked ambition, vacations were all work for her, and money was always tight, yada, yada, yada. That is not what Stacey wanted or needed to hear. Still, she appreciated how Betta and Isaac pitched in with Chloe and Zach. It allowed her more freedom to develop her business, and gave the children a chance to get to know their grandparents. It warmed her heart to see them growing close, even if the Guttons were not the most relaxed, congenial family. Zach and Chloe would never know her parents, so at least they had Grant's, and is was obvious that Betta and Isaac adored all their grandchildren. Babysitting gave their lives meaning beyond the usual routine of out for lunch and shopping for bargains.

Chapter 6

Back at the Ritz Carlton, Stacey was still stupefied with the easy on the eyes, familiar face in front of her. Cas hadn't changed much since high school. Still as trim as a teenager, a little gray around his temples, a few crows feet around his big, grey eyes, but otherwise, there he was: Mr. Tall, Dark, and Handsome. He was never very athletic as Stacey recalled, but all these years later, deep into middle age, he looked to have a seriously flat stomach and youthful, muscular arms, bulging beneath an expensive navy sport coat, everything fitting him as if cut by a tailor. It probably was. He always liked things just so. Stacey liked that about him. He was as sartorial as she was, a rare find.

Memories were flooding back. She recalled how he actually cleaned his bedroom, meticulously. How he sent his jeans to the dry cleaner so that they would have perfect creases down the front. And, how so very much she loved him. She thought he looked like prince charming. And he could be so charming, too. But they were very young, and by his senior year of college, he asked her to "take a break." She remembers not even fully grasping what that request meant. "You mean like over Thanksgiving, not being in touch because your family is traveling?" she asked naively. But a week turned into a month, and then he met Denise, an older, sophisticated, blond senior at a nearby college. All the hurt was flooding back. Denise's family had money and all the things Stacey's didn't. She was well-traveled, well-dressed, cosmopolitan, and in hot pursuit of an engagement ring. A year later they were married.

Some break. More like a whirlwind romance.

Stacey recalled sobbing on the phone to her mother, "Now I know what a broken heart feels like." To that her mom gently assured her, "It will mend."

And soon enough, she met and married Grant. Her mom thought it smelled of a rebound, and cautioned her about jumping in so quickly after her relationship with Cas ended. But even if it was a rebound, it seemed like a good relationship to Stacey. Grant was more attentive than Cas, adored Stacey. Before long they had the big church wedding of her dreams, and a year later, she was expecting Chloe. She would be lying if she said she never thought of Cas, but her life with Grant was solid and good.

"This is a surprise," Stacey mustered, blinking as if in disbelief.

"For sure," said Cas, though he knew otherwise. His years in the IT business provided him with some high-level covert hacking skills, and they were coming in handy.

"Are you still in the Allentown, area? He asked (as if he did not already know).

"Yes, I have a bridal salon there: Golden Day Bridals. This is our annual staff retreat. I try to make the time worth it to the staff by providing a luxurious setting."

"You always had class, Stacey."

Inside Stacey was thinking, *Oh, really now?* Denise's mother was an interior decorator and her own home was a showplace.

She remembered how, after Cas met Denise, he had bragged about his soon to be mother-in-law's finely appointed home. Stacey's home where she grew up was nice, too, but nothing grand. Her mom always believed that if the furniture is not worn out, you keep it. In the little town where she grew up, Stacey remembers feeling proud that their home was not a double home. Most of her friends homes were duplexes, but the Falesh home was a solidly built, single family home, and her dad kept everything in clean, working condition. It might not have been large, or in the least bit stately, but it was nice and comfortable, and her parents pride of ownership was evident. Her mother had an enviable vegetable garden with tomatoes so delicious that Stacey spit out the first store-bought, rubbery tomato she ever ate.

How can they call that tasteless, rubbery ball a tomato?

Denise, on the other hand, came from money, even if it was new money, and her striving, interior-designer mother worked hard at keeping up appearances. A grand piano in the living room, even though no one played it, a spotless twelve seat dining room, though she rarely hosted dinners. But Stacey, always polite, tried hard never to be vindictive or sarcastic.

"Well, thanks, Cas. What brings you to the Ritz-Carlton?" she was biting her tongue just a little.

He seemed a tad disingenuous, but Stacey listened earnestly, trying to be open minded and pleasant. It was a trait that served her especially well in the complicated communication interactions of the bridal business.

"I like stopping by in the evenings before I head home. I live in the city now. The kids are almost grown, just Renee finishing up high school at the Strill School where she boards."

Stacey asked, "How's Denise?" Cas's face froze, and slightly twisted, an expression that Stacey had never remembered.

"You must not have heard. A few years back she passed away. It was a tragic accident," his voice was stoic and flat, as though he had repeated the line many times, bowing his head as he finished.

"Oh, I'm so sorry, I had no idea."

Stacey was embarrassed not to have known, but she wasn't on Facebook, except for the account for Golden Day, and she tried hard to let go of the past, so as to press on for the future. She was mentally trying to add up the number of years since she saw him...twenty?

"How are you? she managed, red-faced and still a little numb that this was even happening.

"I'm okay. Older. Wiser, I hope. It has been a challenge, raising the kids on my own, but they're okay, thank God. The years have been very kind to you, Stacey. You look great."

"You, too Cas," she could feel her cheeks burning. He did look great, in his pastel yellow cashmere sweater under his blazer. He owned yellow. With his black hair and olive skin, he looked like no time had passed.

"Let me buy you a drink," he offered, and before long they were laughing and reminiscing, and Stacey could feel her guard coming down.

She forgot just how long she had known him, how they had practically grown up together. She was fourteen when they met and twenty when he broke it off. He was so handsome, and familiar, they laughed easily about shared college classes, their siblings, and parents and their kids. Cas was making her laugh, recounting the time they got locked in the high school after the maintenance man had shut down the school for the weekend. They had been kissing in the stacks so quietly that the librarian never knew they were there.

"No cell phones back then," Cas reminded her.

"If that happened now it would be nothing to contact someone to pick us up," she added. Cas was always a bit of a phone nerd. He had jimmied the lock on the office door and hacked into the phone system, figuring out how to make an outside call on the elaborate Cisco phone system at their high school. She remembers thinking that if he could get them out of that, he'd be a good husband and father, figuring out life is more difficult situations. It was then, all those years ago, that she started to fall hard for him. She was laughing again at a story he was telling about his daughter Brittany falling off the stage at her first ballet recital.

"Thank goodness she was okay. It brought the house down!" He could always make a mood festive. Cas was fond of her parents, and they were fond of him. It was light and easy to be around Cas, and Stacey couldn't think of the last time she laughed so hard. She remembered thinking how Grant never got to know her parents, and she had wished he had. It would have added a dimension to their relationship that just was not there. She was also reminded of Grant's seriousness. If he wasn't turning down the heat or shutting off the lights he was offering the latest storm report with palpable doom and gloom. He just was not a light guy.

Cas had talked lovingly and brighty about all four of his kids, sharing stories and little personality traits.

Cas said, "Let me see your kids." She scrolled through her photos on her iPhone, and he looked as though he lost his breath.

"Is that Chloe? Oh, my goodness, Stacey, it is YOU again. She is your clone. And Zach, that's Zach? Doesn't he resemble your dad?"

It was true. Chloe really did look exactly like her, and even though she was seventeen, she actually liked the fact that people told her that. She'd post "Twinning with Mom" photos on her Facebook and would comment "Now I know what I'll look like when I'm old!" And Zach did favor her family, too. He had a large, broad head, and a cleft chin, just like her dad. Over the years her sadness of losing her parents was lessened by Chloe and Zach. Stacey's sister Julie would always comment on Zach's "big Falesh head." She felt they were, in some ways, like her parents, only younger. She felt that God had, through them, made them alive again. Not really and truly of course, but in her always optimistic mind she could find solace in the loss of her parents with her flesh and blood, very alive children. She loved thinking about this, and started to well up a bit at the thought.

Blood is thicker than water.

"I loved your parents, Stacey, you know that, don't you? I never knew when they passed. I wished I had. I'm so sorry you have had to raise your family without them."

He pressed her hand. She choked back tears and swallowed hard.

"I've missed you," he said tenderly. "So many times I've thought of you over the years and I never told anyone this, but Brittany, our oldest daughter, always reminded me of you. Where in the world did she get blue eyes?"

Stacey didn't know what to say. He leaned in and kissed her on the lips. She closed her eyes, and her heart melted. In a strange way, seeing Cas again was like seeing family, though she knew that no good could come of this reunion.

Growing up, Cas's family life was a lot like hers, but his parents were younger, more stylish and more concerned with keeping up with others. His father could be critical of his mother, even in front of company, and she remembered Cas, describing his father as someone you would not want to get mad. They were getting on in years now, and Cas, while not exactly estranged, was a poor correspondent.

"Is your sister still in the area?" Stacey asked. She had always liked Cas's sister Cecilia, who had Down's Syndrome.

This forced Cas to share another harsh update, "She passed away last year," he bowed his head.

Cas was good to his sister, and he was close to her, too. She was the same age as Stacey.

"I'm so sorry," Stacey said.

"Yes, it has been very hard on my parents," he added. "I need to visit them more," he added. Stacey's mind was fixated on the death of Cas's wife and his sister and she wondered how he could even handle such shocking blows. She felt ashamed for missing her parents so much.

Life is so fragile, so impermanent.

Chapter 7

Stacey woke up the next morning and closed her eyes again, thinking that she could will the scene that was before her away.

Maybe, somehow it was all a dream.

But when she opened her eyes she saw the devastatingly handsome Cas sleeping next to her, as though it was college. She had been unfaithful to Grant, after twenty years of fidelity. All she could remember was sharing with Cas that she had reserved the Presidential Suite and the next thing she knew they were wrapped in each other's arms, their two bodies a perfect fit, like no years had passed. The tenderness was borne from so much shared history, so much longing that neither of them were willing to admit. Deep down, she had missed Cas, too. She just never let her mind go there. Her answer to all that ailed her: work, work, and work some more. But right now, she was in Cas's arms, in a plush hotel room in a glittering city, and the reality of the situation jolted her not only out of bed, but into the absurdity of what had just happened.

This is how a perfectly good life gets messed up.

"Cas, you need to leave. My team will be up in an hour for our morning brainstorming session."

"Is that how you greet me after the evening we shared?" he playfully asked, pulling her close to him. One thing she knew for sure: the Cas Ferraro charms were still firmly in place. She lingered on his handsome face, his playful expression and the deep connection she was feeling. But she was also a fiercely task oriented, do the right thing woman, and she had to set up boundaries and be firm.

"No, I mean it. This was a mistake. I let myself get caught up in some very old feelings that were better left alone."

She was quickly dressing and imploring him to leave. He was still stretched out on the luxurious down bed immobile and unpersuaded by her pleas, all flat stomach and olive skin. Stacey tried to be forceful and dramatic:

"Please leave, and never contact me again," her voice was stressed, but resolute.

"You don't mean that," Cas looked wounded and yet happy as if reveling in what just happened, his big gray eyes in mocking frightful disbelief, more soulful than any Frank Sinatra era crooner.

"I do, Cas. I'm maaaarried, and I want to keep it that way. What we had was ages ago and we need to leave it there. Please understand," she pleaded.

"Okay, I understand. I'm gone," he said and quickly dressed and left with a kiss on her cheek.

He turned to her and locked eyes with her, and said, as if to remind her of something that she needed to know, with his right finger pointed up: "I'll always love you," he half-whispered as he pulled the door quietly behind him. Stacey sat down on the edge of the bed, her hand on her mouth, her head bowed in shame and disbelief, and her heart at once felt aching and full.

What just happened?

Nancy, Martin and Lisa would be up in less than a half hour. She quickly leaped up, ordered room service—coffee and breakfast for four—jumped into the shower and got dressed. She was good at pushing her emotions to the back and if ever there was a need, this was the time to do it. She turned on the television to get her mind elsewhere and was riveted by the breaking story on *Right Now*, her favorite network morning program. The girl next door host, Rachel Marston, was tearing up as she delivered the shocking news. Her long time co-host, the avuncular Chad Brown, was fired the previous evening when a female employee came forward with sexual assault charges.

Her voice cracking, her famous dimples nowhere to be seen, she said, "It is heartbreaking to learn that my good friend, and longtime partner on *Right Now* will no longer be here. While I'm dismayed by the news, I am also proud of the woman who had the courage to speak out." Stacey could not believe it. She'd been watching Chad Brown on *Right Now* show since Chloe was a baby, and even went to a live studio taping once.

Chad Brown? What is the world coming to?

She needed all the strength and focus she could muster to charge forward with the work at hand. Onward with Golden Day Bridals Strategic Planning. Luckily the suite was spacious and the pocket doors closed off the bedroom area. She didn't want anyone noticing the bed as rumpled as it was, or that all the pillows seemed used. She could just see Lisa looking curiously with the thought in her head all over her face: How could one person use all those pillows on that mammoth bed? Lisa could be especially nosy.

Chapter 8

Like clockwork, Nancy, Lisa and Martin all came knocking at precisely the same time. They all looked as though they had slept well, especially Martin. He was another sharp dresser, and he took such good care of himself. No one ever guessed he was closing in on seventy. He showed up smelling good, his couture cut gray-white hair still damp, in his Loro Piana knit sportcoat.

Something Cas would wear.

She needed to forget about Cas and focus on this session.

Stacey opened her laptop and, ever helpful, Martin suggested they review the previous strategic plan from two years ago to reflect on where they have been before they discuss the goals for the next two years.

"Great idea, thanks" Stacey said.

She was especially grateful for his penetrating thinking and focus now, since she felt completely off her game. Even though he was her employee, Martin was the closest thing Stacey had to a brother. They had a familial-like chemistry that just clicked from the first moment they met at a bridal show. He was editor of a valley-wide lifestyle magazine, that was losing readership, and they kept in touch. When the magazine closed three years later, Stacey offered him a sales consultant position at Golden Day. He was great for business. He knew everyone in the Lehigh Valley and he was a hard worker and a loyal friend. Not only were they simpatico, he was fabulous with the customers. He was intuitive about designs that would suit both mother and daughter, and kept sessions cordial, and fun, even when it seemed that World War III was about to erupt over a fitted gown or a ball gown, or some other hot button style-related issue. Impressed with his knowledge of styles, enthusiasm, charisma, and appearance, producers of *You've Got To Buy That Dress!* started to inquire if Martin could appear on the show too. Stacey was happy to share the limelight, since it was getting to be too much for her to make weekly trips into New York City.

Surveying the expansive digs, Nancy joked, "Oh, this is how the other half lives," as she took in the spoilings of the Presidential Suite.

Lisa said, "Well, we aren't exactly suffering in our rooms, but wow, this is NICE," she said as she poured herself a cup of coffee and opened up her folder.

Stacey said, "Team, it has been a great year. So much has happened that has been unexpected. Good, unexpected," she corrected herself, feeling a bit self conscience. "Our numbers are ridiculous, really good. Let's get started."

They worked until almost noon without even looking up. Stacey brought up the proposal from the downtown Allentown Development Authority. The downtown was picking up in recent years, and Golden Day Bridals was offered a half-price deal on a five thousand square foot showroom, right next to the hockey arena if they would move within three months from their location three miles west of downtown. With the half price deal, The Neighborhood Improvement Zone, known as the NIZ, was making it tempting. People are coming downtown for the shows at the arena and the new restaurants, and Golden Day Bridals was a destination shop that would continue to bring people downtown. The NIZ administrators were making the deal sweet because they knew the value of Golden Day Bridals to continue the revitalization downtown. The staff liked the idea of a whole new shop. There would be a new branding campaign, and the bigger space would mean that everyone would have an office. Being downtown meant they could walk to good restaurants for lunch, and they'd be close to shopping and nightlife too. It was a real step-up for everyone in the salon.

Stacey announced, "Break time," and asked to reconvene over lunch at one at the hotel restaurant, Aquimero. Lisa immediately announced that she wanted to walk to Independence Mall, and Nancy joined her. Martin wanted to people watch at the pool and relax with a good glass of top-shelf Scotch, and Stacey was relieved for some time with her thoughts. She was, what she liked to call, an introverted extrovert. She loved meeting and greeting, spending time with clients and new vendors, but after a couple of hours, she craved solitude. With her growing business, the kids and their friends, her in-laws coming and going, there was almost no time in her life for alone time. Sometimes she would just go into the bathroom and sit on the toilet seat just to be alone.

Does Wonder Woman sit on the toilet seat for 'me time?'

But as soon as the team left her suite, all she could say to herself was, No, no, no, no. What did I do? Being alone with her thoughts now, was no solace.

How could I have let that happen?

She knew that risking everything with an old flame was dangerous and stupid. Her life was just getting good, the stress of raising children was slowly receding as Chloe and Zach got older and more independent, and money was less of an issue now that Golden Day was flourishing.

She was startled from her thoughts with the sound of

her phone. Probably Lisa and Nancy asking her to come to the Liberty Bell or something.

She looked down at an unfamiliar number: She read: "Thank you for that, Stacey. You are so beautiful, and I hope we can keep in touch." Stacey froze and closed her eyes in horror as she wondered how Cas got her phone number. She quickly deleted the text, touched up her make-up and went outside for some much-needed fresh air and a brisk walk.

It wasn't just any old flame. It was Cas.

Chapter 9

The sales rep from Nera Savoy, Courtney Phillips, was joining the team for lunch with the book of new designs that was hot off the press. Stacey could not wait to see them. The new trend of lace sleeves had replaced the strapless look, and Stacey was thrilled about it.

What made all women think they could pull off the strapless look?

It was so uncomfortable to tell brides that covering their arms would give them a nicer look in photos and that twenty years later, when they were looking back at their photos, they would be happy with the advice. Princess Kate was to thank for the new modest, lace bridal dresses, and Stacey was eager to see Nera Savoy's always innovative interpretations.

Maybe more than that, she was happy to have her mind focused on something other than Cas.

They met at one of the white linen topped tables, grandly set for an upscale lunch, with the aroma of the fresh lillies wafting through the air. Stylish Courtney opened the book to reveal the latest looks. The new dresses were stunning. Immediately, Stacey was drawn to the Illusion Bodice Wedding Dress. What she and her bride's loved most about Nera Savoy's designs was that they seemed effortlessly feminine. The Eliana dress took Stacey's breath away. The empire waist would take twenty pounds off any bride. She ordered a half a million in dresses, and Courtney, grateful for the big sale, included delivery direct from their

Madison Avenue flagship store. Martin gave Lisa and Nancy a big eyed look when he realized the price tag, and Lisa winked back, suggesting that an order this size can only mean one thing: Stacey plans to move the store to the larger location downtown.

Just as Courtney finished computing the order, lunch was served. Delicious coastal Latin cuisine and nobody was shy about ordering up. Martin and Lisa ordered shrimp cocktail appetizers and the wood fired steak. Stacey and Nancy had the ceviche bar and Courtney had ribs. It was absolutely delectable, and Stacey enjoyed treating the team. What she always thought was great about Nancy, Lisa and Martin, is that whether she ordered in Yocco hot dogs for lunch or this feast at the Ritz, they were always grateful and always giving 100% for Golden Day. Stacey loved being a business owner, especially now when things were going so well.

"Would you like to see a dessert menu?" the waiter asked.

As if on cue, all five said, "No, thanks!" It was true, that even though it was upscale dining, the portions were generous, and no one had room for dessert. Stacey was starting to feel grateful that there was no scale in her room.

I'll weigh myself first thing when I get home. Skip dinner tonight.

Stacey took in the scene and smiled, and as if he knew there was a pause in the action, her phone buzzed with another text message from Cas. "Do you have time for a nightcap tonight?"

This time Stacey texted back: "No. Not tonight, not ever. Please stop texting me."

"What is it?" Nancy asked, as if she perceived some issue from the look on Stacey's face. "Everything OK at home?"

"Yes, of course," Stacey lied, "Just Zach trying to test the limits of Grant's patience as usual."

The team had one more night and after lunch it was time for more strategic planning. Stacey suggested they relax for an hour or so and meet up in her suite later that afternoon. Martin made a beeline for the lobby bar where he'd hoped to meet new people. He was always networking, and if it didn't turn into business for Golden Day, it would be a contact for himself. Unlike most people past sixty, Martin increased his circle of friends and acquaintances. Lisa and Nancy both went back to their rooms, and Stacey thanked Courtney for joining them for lunch, the special attention, and for the good deals for Golden Day. The dresses would be a fabulous addition to the already increasing inventory.

Stacey headed to her suite, too, but before she got there her phone rang. She answered.

"Stacey, let me see you tonight. I miss you already," Cas said.

Now Grant was trying to call her. She disconnected Cas's call and breezily asked, "Hey, how are things going?" to Grant. "Good. My parents took the kids to Costco. That ought to tire them out. Miss you honey. What time do you think you'll be home tomorrow?" he asked.

"Not too late. Maybe four or five. It has been a productive weekend. Love you, G."

"Love you, doll."

From the moment they met, Grant took to calling Stacey "Doll" and even though some would say that's awfully retro, and maybe even anti-feminist, she loved it. She hung up and her mind turned to Cas. She needed to tell him it was a one time deal and that he must stay away. She dialed his number but before she could finish dialing, he was standing in front of her.

She needed to be direct: "Cas, this has to stop. I'm married. Happily married. I know we had something great, but that was a long time ago. I want to keep my marriage together. Please don't come here anymore."

He looked hurt and even a little angry. "Fine. Goodbye. But I know Grant doesn't make you happy. You can live in your make-believe world, but what we had last night was magical and you know it."

With that he walked out the door of the hotel. Shaken, Stacey went up to her room and sat on the edge of the bed wondering what just happened. She said a quick prayer, asking God for guidance:

Dear Lord, strengthen me.

Before long the team appeared, and despite being distracted and stressed out, Stacey directed the group through a powerful strategic planning session. It was clear that at the end of it, expansion of the salon's physical space, an ever-expanding brand presence, and continued publicity on a national level, would be keys to capitalize on the growth of Golden Day Bridals. Stacey wanted to include the innovative new designs coming each day from a growing array of Israeli designers. The lace treatments and expertly crafted silhouettes were absolutely stunning, and Golden Day would be the only bridal salon in the tri-state area to have an international perspective in bridal dresses. In addition to gowns from leading international designers, Stacey felt committed about providing brides with the finest gowns made in the USA, as well. Each bride who ordered a gown from Golden Day could also have custom changes and exquisite alterations so that the gown fit her perfectly. Whether a bride wants a Cinderella ball gown, a fit and flair trumpet, to a chic, edgy modern dress, and whether she is a size double zero or a thirty-two, Golden Day is the place for her dreams to come true, and with a new location, a dizzying array of inventory would be at her fingertips.

It was almost evening, and the team opted to have "dinner on their own." They loved being a team, but they worked hard during the session, were tired and in need of some alone time. Stacey was happy to retreat to her suite and sort out her emotions, the upcoming move, and to check in with Grant and the kids. She made a note to call the realtor and to put the new location plans in motion. She drew a long bath, put on her spa robe, and phoned room service. When her pasta and vegetables arrived, she climbed into bed to eat while reviewing her notes for tomorrow.

Grant FaceTimed her with Chloe and Grant in the background, doing their homework in the kitchen.

Guilt washed over her.

"We're managing, but we really miss you," Grant said.

"Love you, Mom!" the kids sang.

"What time do you think you'll be back on Monday?" Grant asked.

Normally it grated on Stacey's nerves how Grant would try to pin her down to a time that she would be returning from a trip. It made her nervous, like if she was ten minutes later than she estimated, she'd better call him and tell him.

But this time when he asked, she realized how good it felt to have people who love her enough to wonder what time she will be home.

What am I doing? I have the best family in the world.

And yet Stacey knew that while she really screwed up here, no one person is all good or all bad. Some very good people have done some very bad things and some very bad people had a lot of goodness in them, too. She opened up the mini bar, stocked with wine and goodies, and shoved a dark chocolate candy bar into her mouth, swirled it around, and then spit it out. She did the same for the bag of potato chips, pretzels and the little chocolate cake. She threw the vegetables and pasta into the garbage before she could eat that, too.

This will be my dinner. I hope I'm not gaining weight.

Chapter 10

It was six when Stacey awoke on her own. She never needed an alarm to awaken her; she had a natural clock, and being an "early to bed" person, she simply awoke when rested. She texted the team to meet for breakfast at eight. "Parting Thoughts" she called it. Martin, Lisa and Nancy appeared at breakfast with stories of their past evening events.

Lisa, recently divorced, had hung out at the bar hoping to meet someone, but gave up by 10. "I'm getting too old for this," she lamented, even though she was barely forty. "I seem to be attracting the sixty-plus set, which, sorry Martin, is super depressing. Like what is up with that?"

Martin didn't mind the dig. He had met someone, a retired dentist, who had a farm in Doylestown and he had high hopes. "We are meeting there next weekend," he said, with school boy anticipation.

Like Stacey, Nancy had turned in early. Leave it to Martin to have made a connection. "Always networking," Nancy teased him, then added, "In my book, honey, nothing beats a bubble bath in a luxury hotel, and I mean nothing!"

Everyone laughed.

Over breakfast Stacey said that they could expect a move, and that she would be calling the realtor. It would be a big step, but the time is right to be all in at Golden Day Bridals. It would be an exciting year ahead with a new, big location downtown and increased visibility in the press.

They gathered their luggage, and Martin drove them back to the Lehigh Valley. It had been a productive retreat. Goals had been set and the team felt pampered in the meantime. It was a good yearly ritual, but Nancy could sense that Stacey was off her game.

"You seem distracted," Nancy said to Stacey. "No, no, it's just a lot to get in motion," Stacey said, and they all seemed to relax, riding silently for the hour trip home.

When they got to the salon, Nancy handed a little gift bag to Stacey, "for Chloe's birthday, just a little something, from Aunt Nancy," and Martin gave her a little birthday care package of what looked like a nail file, lip balm, and hand cream for Chloe, too. "Tell her to keep this in her backpack," Martin said.

Wait till Chloe sees. Aunt Nancy and Uncle Martin are so sweet. I have the best team in the world.

"Love you, all. Thanks for all you do for me and for Golden Day," Stacey said, and with that, the team went straight to their cars, except Stacey who went inside to tackle some paperwork and to make a few calls to brides who needed to come in to pick up their dresses after their final fittings.

Before she realized what time it was, her cell phone was ringing. Grant asked, "You almost back?"

"Yes, I'll be home in thirty minutes," she said and she finished up, packed up her work tote bag, and headed home to Grant and the kids. She was glad to be back home.

It will be a long time before I go to Philadelphia again. That's a city I need to stay away from.

Chapter 11

Chloe, Zach, and Grant greeted Stacey when she walked in the door. "I made you roasted vegetables and quinoa," Grant said.

Stacey was touched. Grant rarely cooked, but they had begun getting fresh food in boxed meals each week from Veggie Fresh, and Grant found it easy to follow the directions and make nice dinners when Stacey wasn't home. He complained about the cost, but he enjoyed the food, and Stacey liked the hand up in getting dinner on the table. All the ingredients for inspired meals and none of the shopping or the thinking about it. And the less thinking about food that Stacey did, the less obsessed she would be.

The kids both hugged her. "We missed you, Mom," Zach said. For teenagers, Chloe and Zach were awfully affectionate. Being away even for just the long weekend sharpened her appreciation for how grown up both Chloe and Zach looked, especially Chloe. Taller than her, and more slender than Stacey had ever been, even at that age, Chloe's thick, virgin chestnut hair fell below her waist. She asked for highlights, but Stacey held firm, wishing she had never started lightening her own hair to the point of looking basically blond.

Once you start playing with the color, you might as well move into the beauty parlor for all the upkeep it takes.

Her eyes were Stacey's -- huge, blue saucers--and her little turned up nose, no one could trace where it came from. Without ever having braces, her perfect smile was gleaming white. She was beautiful, and the best part was, she had no idea. She wasn't into make-up, didn't ask for expensive clothes, and was pretty chill… for a teenage girl. She was happy to reuse her old backpack and would even wear Stacey's hand me downs if they fit.

Zach was somehow taller than everyone. Close to six feet, he looked like a young version of her dad, but he also had a few Gutton features, like the Roman nose, which suited his broad face. When he was a toddler, a complete stranger, a fashion photographer, approached her on the street and asked if he could pose for an ad for a now defunct department store downtown, Glass's. With his ear to ear smile, and thick mop of brown hair, he made an adorable model. The yellowing ad still hangs in her shop, and she is so proud to say, "That's my son!" to anyone who would listen, recounting how he was scouted off the street. She marveled at how she and Grant created such kind-hearted, unspoiled and good-looking children. And she was touched the way they truly worried about her when she went away, even just for a few days, even when she wasn't that far from home. She didn't know how parents who traveled abroad for extended amounts of time did it. She just hated to be away from her family.

Instantly she was awash with guilt over what happened with Cas. She thought about all she had and what she was risking.

"Anything new happen while I was gone?" she asked.

"No, same old. My parents came for a couple of days to pitch in," Grant said.

"Pop-Pop wants to sell the Florida condo," Zach said, "but Granny doesn't," he added.

The house looked good. Grant was not a slob, his biggest infraction was reusing paper coffee cups from the local Barista Cafe. He called it recycling, but Stacey found it truly gross the way he lined up the old, used paper coffee cups next to the sink. She despised drinking from paper cups and really hated clutter, so this habit of Grant's really got under her skin. She tried to throw away the cups, but Grant seemed to have a photographic memory about how many were lined up and would call her on it.

"Oh, do you know a Mary Ann Redds from Bishop Frances High School?" Grant asked. "She called while you were gone, and asked specifically for you to call her back by Tuesday."

Stacey thought it was just reunion round-up time. Of course they always try to get as many alumni to come to the reunions as possible. Since she graduated, she had not been back for any reunions. Just too busy raising kids, growing the business. She felt badly about it, but she didn't think she'd actually go to the reunion coming up either.

"I wish I actually enjoyed seeing people from high school, but I just don't," Stacey said. "I haven't kept in touch with anyone, so who would I be thrilled to see?" she asked to no one in particular.

Grant said, "Don't look at me. You know I dread things like that. You won't get an argument here. But you should call Mary Ann back. She was very nice on the phone."

Stacey's mind returned to Bishop Frances High School and it lingered on Cas. Except for him all of a sudden now, she really did not keep in touch with old classmates. They probably posted every happy moment of their lives on Facebook, while their true existence was hanging by threads, full of resentments and resistance. All toothy grins in front of the fireplace for the Christmas card, and next year they're taking loans from their 401K to pay the divorce attorney.

Not for me. Onward.

Stacey picked at her food as they ate, and she shared that Golden Day Bridal Salon planned to expand downtown. Grant thought it could be a good move, but he was worried about the cost. The current location wasn't fancy, but it was cheap, and it was a huge step up from the basement beginnings. They bought the half-double house at a real bargain, successfully petitioned the township to run a business from it, and the mortgage was almost paid in full. The last time Grant checked the value on an online real estate site it had doubled in price. They had bought it at just the right time. The new location would be a rental, and even with the half price offer, the rent would be double the mortgage payment. But the new location would be so much bigger and better, with so much more inventory, that it should more than offset the cost. Grant's office is downtown, and Stacey thought that maybe they could carpool.

After years of deterioration and very few businesses, everything was on the upswing in downtown Allentown. Funky, eclectic coffee shops, trendy advertising agencies, and at least a dozen new high-end restaurants opened in the past year. Downtown Allentown was coming back, and Stacey and Golden Day would be able to get in on prime real estate if she acted fast. Grant offered to review the contract and go check out the new location with Stacey. He was cautiously supportive and wanted to make sure that financially it was a sound move.

Zach asked if he could go to the basketball game at the high school, and without any complaint about the cost of gas, or how many miles it was from their remote home, surprisingly Grant offered to drive.

I think he actually missed me.

Stacey looked at Grant softly with gratitude as he left with Zach, his recycled paper coffee cup filled to the brim, and a copy of the latest Consumer Watch magazine to study while he waited. Zach was at the age where it was totally uncool to be seen at a high school sporting event with either parent, and he even resented Grant waiting outside while he watched the game, but there was no way Grant would do two round trips in one night, and he seemed to enjoy sitting outside in the cold van, bundled up in his winter coat, sipping hot coffee, listening to music and reading. Chloe invited her friend Elena over, and Stacey cleaned up from dinner, organized her paperwork for the coming week, and tried to push what happened with Cas out of her mind.

At least he has not contacted me again. I pray he got the message.

Stacey opened her computer, went straight to her email, and there it was: an email from Cas. "Dear Stacey, Hope you made it home safely. Your idea to move your shop downtown is great. I say go for it. When I moved my business to a more visible location, business doubled. If you want to discuss it with me, let me know. Remember, it is all about ROI. Wonderful to see you again. Let's keep in touch. Love Always, Cas."

Love Always? On my work email!?

Stacey lost her breath for a moment. *What was this breezy tone about? And how did Cas know we discussed moving Golden Day downtown?And how did he get my email address?*

Stacey's mind was reeling. She found his chatty "hey girl" tone completely unsettling.

Get off my email. Get out of my life!

She could not remember ever discussing any of this with him. She closed her eyes and tried to think what to do. This wasn't just going to "go away," Cas seems determined to keep in touch.

Pushing it out of her mind, Stacey went downstairs, poured herself a big glass of Chardonnay, and started in on the proposal for the new location and the grant from the Neighborhood Improvement Zone, or the NIZ as everyone called it. She reached for the folder from the real estate agent and remembered that she must have left it at her office by mistake. She hated when she did that, and usually just waited until the morning to deal with it. Having Cas back in her life made her a scatterbrain, and she needed to be focused for the move and for her family.

I'm so stupid! I really need to get going on this.

She tried to call Grant to see if he could stop by the salon on his way home and pick up the folder, but he wasn't answering his phone. He had the annoying habit of shutting off his cell, something about preserving the life of the battery. She grabbed a big chocolate chip cookie, and one of Grant's paper cups as she headed toward the garage, jumped into her SUV and drove quickly to get to Golden Day. Her mind was racing and confused about Cas, and she thought that if she could finish the proposal tonight, she could drop it off tomorrow. It would get the ball rolling. Anxiously she chewed the giant, sweet treat and spit it out into the cup.

Action beats inaction. Do, do, do.

One of her favorite mantras.

Chapter 12

The usual thirty-minute trip to Golden Day seemed like it took five minutes. Stacey was a woman on a mission. She knew once she had the grant proposal framework from the folder, she'd have the proposal done in an hour. She ran up the steps to her salon and noticed a light coming from the back office.

That's so weird.

She surmised that she just left it on before, although she tried to keep the back lights off, especially since the showroom light was on all night for both security reasons and to showcase a dress of the week. One of the advantages of the current location, is that is was completely safe. Located in a small residential area, with just a few other small businesses, the twin home was nestled between astute "neighborhood watch" type neighbors. Adding to that, the owner of the other half of the building had a pitbull, Sandy, that barked her head off if anyone unknown entered. It sometimes scared customers to hear a dog barking, one of the reasons she wanted to move the salon, but it was highly effective for security. As she entered she noticed a few of her business cards from the counter on the floor, picked them up, and then went to her office for the folder. She was sure it was on her desk, but when she got there, it was nowhere to be found.

Are you kidding me?

So tired from the weekend, and the emotional impact of seeing Cas, the last thing she needed was this extra trip in the car. She looked at the family photo on her desk and lingered on it.

How did that happen--the kids so grown up?I'm an idiot for what I did. I'm a bad person.

And then she noticed that the most recent photo of Chloe had a big crack on the glass covering her image. She hadn't noticed it before and she just put the photo in the frame.

Maybe the cleaning crew dropped it. Odd.

Chloe really did look just like her and her latest school photo was absolutely gorgeous. She was all grown up, her silky, long brunette hair framing her full face, replete with dimples and those huge blue eyes. Stacey scoured her office, trying to look for the folder when her cell phone rang.

She tensed up.

It was Grant. "I just got home. Where are you?" he asked. When Stacey explained that she had gone back to her office for the NIZ folder, Grant chided her. "You were gone all weekend, Stacey. I was hoping we could relax together tonight," he sounded wounded.

That was how he asked for sex these days. He'd say "Let's relax together."

"I'm sorry, Grant, I just felt motivated to get this done, but I can't even find the folder. So frustrating," she said. She got back into her van and headed home.

Chapter 13

As she got into her car, she could see her phone lighting up again. "Grant, I said, I'm on my way," she said as she picked up the phone without even looking at it.

"Is that how you speak to your dearly beloved husband?"

Stacey froze. She almost hit the car in front of her.

"Cas, you can't call me. Please stop this," she said.

"I need to see you, Stacey," he said. "We both know we have more together than you have with Grant, and you know I love you more," he said. "Tell me you didn't feel the connection," he continued. "I will always love you. I never stopped," he added.

"Cas, I'm happily married. I have children. I have a good life. What we had all those years ago is over," she said.

"I need you to look me in the eye and tell me that," Cas said. "Meet me for lunch tomorrow, please," he said.

"I don't think that's a good idea," Stacey said. "Why are you doing this now? Before our kids were born, I thought of you every day. You broke up with *me*, remember?" she pleaded. "I hurt, Cas. You broke my heart. But too much time has passed. This is over. I made a happy life for myself," she said.

"Just meet me for lunch. No strings. I just want to talk to you face to face," he said.

The truth is she wanted to see him. But everything she told him is also true: the time had passed for a relationship.

She made a good, decent, and happy life for herself, and she was proud of her family, her business, and where her life was headed. Getting caught up with Cas was a terrible idea, and though her head was telling her to stay away, deep down she wanted to see him again. He got to her when he spoke of her parents. It reminded her of a time when she wasn't an orphan. When she had parents who cared about her, listened to her, looked out for her. She remembers when she understood, from her own lived experiences, that blood was thicker than water.

"OK,' Stacey relented. "Meet me downtown, at Casa Mia, the new Italian place, at noon."

With that she hung up and pulled into the driveway. She caught a glimpse of herself in the rearview mirror and gave a foreboding look.

Grant was waiting for her at the door with a look of disdain, his mouth turned down because of the "one hour round-trip, probably ten dollars in gas," she had spent to go back to get the folder.

As their marriage matured, she found herself wishing Grant would love her more passionately and less practically, sometimes thinking that maybe if he were much older than she was he would find her ways somehow adorable. She wished even just once Grant would keep all the lights in their relationship on, so to speak, to prove that he loved her and that she really could do no wrong. They didn't have the kind of marriage where Grant might joke, "Happy Wife, Happy Life." The older Grant got, the more he harped on the most mundane details of day-to-day living. Her mind lingered on how handsome and manly Cas looked.

I'm playing with fire.

Chapter 14

Stacey got up early and continued her hunt for the elusive NIZ folder. "You're up early," Grant said. He was in a good mood. "Oh, lots to do, and I still haven't found the folder," she said. "I guess I'll pick up another one from the NIZ office later," she added. "I can get one for you, the office is right next to our building," Grant offered. He was always so quick to run errands like that, and Stacey appreciated it. Because he could just walk over to the NIZ office, it wouldn't cost him anything.

"Thanks, that would be great," Stacey said, thinking that even though she was meeting Cas near Grant's company, he rarely left his office to go to lunch. But this sneaking around thing was tricky. If, in fact, he walked over to the NIZ office at lunch time, they could run into each other. Stacey pushed it out of her mind think that it would still be unlikely. Rarely did Grant left his office at lunchtime, unless corporate reps were in town, and they would not be back for weeks.

She could hear Zach and Chloe arguing upstairs. They got along really well as kids, and many people even took them as twins, but as they moved into their teen years, Zach's gloomy disposition often set the tone for family vacations and outings, and Chloe was growing tired of it. Zach would start picking on Chloe for no real reason, just because he was cranky.

"I hate that song, its so stupid," Stacey could hear Zach saying.

"You're stupid," Chloe retorted. "I'm not the one in remedial algebra," he shot back.

"OK, kids, stop it," Grant yelled up stairs. "Come down for breakfast, and get packed up for school." They bounded down the steps.

Chloe looked at Stacey, "You look nice, mom," she said. "I like your boots."

Stacey blushed. Had she really stepped up her look subconsciously because of her lunch with Cas?

Grant chimed in a rare dramatic voice, "Yes, I'm definitely glad you bought that dress!" he mocked the TV show.

"Stacey, did you call Mary Ann Redds back from Bishop Frances? I see she called again," and he pressed the button on the antiquated answering machine.

"Hi Stacey. It's Mary Ann Redds. Not sure if you remember me. From Bishop Frances? I wanted to wait to speak with you, but I'm having trouble reaching you. Anyway, the committee voted, and you are the recipient of the Bishop Frances Alumni Award for Professional Achievement. We all see you on *You've Got To Buy That Dress!* and well, you are the most famous alumna. We hope you will come to the reunion next month and receive your award. Please call me back when you can. Thanks and congratulations!"

"Wow, Mom, that's kind of cool," said Chloe. "

Yea, congrats, Mom," Zach said.

Grant beamed, "I'm married to a famous alumna. But I knew that. I think we should all go to see you accept your award. That's great, honey. I'm so proud of you," Grant said sincerely. And with that Stacey, smiling ear to ear, and the kids, piled into her Golden Day/mom mobile, and Grant left for his office.

When she got to the salon, Nancy met her at the door. "Oh, my God, Stacey, Bailey Grift's scheduler called. She's getting married and she wants a private consultation for her wedding gown."

Bailey Grift, the international pop superstar who was born and raised (well *raised* until age fifteen and international stardom catapulted her to the top of the charts and on the cover of every magazine) in the rolling countryside of Berks Township.

"The only way they will confirm to use Golden Day is if we can provide complete anonymity," Nancy added.

Bailey Grift's latest blockbuster, "I had to do it," was a backlash against the male gaze and the harassment that she experienced in her career in pop. It was completely in sync with the growing #MeToo phenomenon. Women were sick and tired of being objectified, and this young sensation was a heroine for the cause.

Stacey was thrilled for the opportunity, and made a note to return the call after her current appointment, a mother-daughter duo staring at her to get started on their appointment, the daughter taking selfies to post to social media #gettinghitched.

Funny how some people want attention for one thing and privacy for another.

It was another packed day. The local public television station would be coming in to shoot footage for an upcoming program about local women entrepreneurs.

Chapter 15

During the interview for the entrepreneur program, Stacey mentioned her upcoming alumni award, and it did bring her joy. The reporter asked her to paint a picture of young Stacey Falesh. She asked: "Where did your drive come from?" Stacey recounted feeling completely out of her league at Bishop Frances. Most of the other kids came from more academic backgrounds, and her friends at Bishop Frances had grand family outings like cruises over the Christmas holiday, and summers at the beach. It was a world Stacey simply could not relate to; her family never even took one vacation. Ever. She recalled when her friend Gina told her that her family was going to Europe, Stacey's first reaction was that someone in her family must be sick, and they were going to Italy to provide family support. But what Stacey lacked in connections and money, she made up for in sheer determination. Maybe her grit and gumption were finally paying off.

When she finished the interview, she could see Martin studying her face. There is no hiding from Martin. He could sense something was wrong and she could see him trying to come up with something to say to ask her if everything is OK. Martin. Stacey really grew to appreciate him. He could be the strangest person in so many ways, and Zach even pleaded with Stacey not to leave him alone with Martin. Not that Martin tried anything untoward, but he was so forceful in suggesting how Zach could make his future brighter. "Get to know others," Martin would say, and "be a sharp dresser!" It was not anything Martin was not practicing himself. He seemed ubiquitous in the local newspaper social page, representing Golden Day at every Rotary or Chamber of Commerce meeting in town. And he was always more put together than most of the women at the events. Stacey and Martin clicked the minute they met. It was as if they had known each other their whole lives. He would tease her in a way that was never suggestive of anything but a deep affinity and friendship for her. She tried to be as good of a friend to him, and through Golden Day she could be: days off, any perk she could offer him, she did. He made up for it double in loyalty and business. The mothers and daughters loved him. He was the most requested sales associate. Today, Stacey, thought, she'd ask him if he'd like to be featured on *You've Got To Buy That Dress!* if her schedule got too crazy.

"Hey Martin!" Stacey enthused as she walked in.

"Your hair looks great!" he said back. "Got a hot date?"

Not funny.

"Martin?" "Yes, little one?" He called her that a lot because of their height difference. He was "Big Martin" to many of his long time friends. He stood 6'4" and kept himself trim and slim, often announcing his morning's weight to whoever would listen.

"175 today!" he said.

"And I was 135 today, Martin. Trying to keep the number down."

"Atta girl! You look good!" he said. Martin was always good for positive reinforcement. Stacey did not want to think about the amount of mental energy she spent both thinking about food and trying to stay slim, or about how much she chewed and spit off-limit foods. Martin's cobblers were no help. "Live big and stay small" was a mantra she would repeat to herself over and over again when faced with the "all you can eat" breakfasts on her buying trips. She knew she could be really fat if she just ate what she really wanted to all of the time, and no walk at home video for thirty minutes in the morning would erase that. Martin shared the same underlying terror about getting fat as Stacey did. The difference is that Martin was thin by nature, with no eating issues. He just had to put the fork down. Stacey thought about food all the time, and when she sought therapy from a well-known eating disorder expert, she was told that she wasn't eating enough. Doubtful, but hopeful for a cure, Stacey gave it a week to eat normally -- six times a day -- the therapist told her. But when she weighed herself at the end of the week the scale read 138. She went back to her heavily restrictive diet and tried not to chew and spit, but once her weight was down to 135 again, she couldn't seem to stop herself. Martin suspected she had a problem, but it was the one area, and possibly the only thing he not only didn't know much about, so he felt it better left unsaid. Martin often took out the trash to be helpful, and could smell the sugary sweets wafting through the air. Once he asked why she "threw out" his blueberry cobbler. Stacey wanted to come clean and tell her she "threw up" the cobbler, but she didn't want to burden Martin. Yet if there was anyone she could tell, it would be Martin.

When she was nervous about her first European buying trip on her own, he assured her that the time alone would do her good. "You take care of everyone all the time. Don't serve the time, let the time serve you. Eat healthy, get plenty of sleep, drink water. Use it as a mini-spa vacation," he encouraged. Martin was a true friend.

"Martin, with the move downtown, I'm going to be very busy next month and *You've Got To Buy That Dress!*

already requested five appearances. How do you feel about appearing on the show? The producers think you'd be terrific," she said. Without any hesitation, almost as though he'd be waiting to be asked, he smiled ear to ear and said, "I'd love to!" That was it. She'd call the producers and let them know. She had a good team, and she knew it. "That would be great, Martin, thank you. I may be a bit long at lunch today. Running downtown. Will you be sure to stay in and take care of anyone who might drop in?"

"You've got it. No problem, Stacey. I packed my homemade potato soup, anyway. It is soup weather already," he said. He locked eyes with her: "Everything OK, kiddo?"

She said quickly, "Yep, just a lot of balls in the air."

"That's part of making it to the big time, kid. Let me know if there is anything else you need, OK?" and he gave her a comforting look. "And I put some of my homemade blueberry cobbler in the back for all of you," he added. Martin could cook and bake better than anyone.

"Yum!" she said, as Lisa and Nancy appeared.

The phone rang, and like everyone did when they picked up, Lisa sang into the phone, "It's another golden day and Golden Day Bridals. How may I help you?" Stacey walked back to her office, taking in the intoxicating aroma of the cobbler, she resisted slicing a piece off, and smiled to herself about how good things were going with the salon. When she saw the NIZ folder right on the top of her desk, she lost her breath.

That was not here last night. I tore this office apart looking for it.

"Martin, did you put the folder on my desk?" she asked.

"No, Stacey. I wasn't even in your office today," he said. Stacey got an uneasy feeling in her stomach. She could not imagine how it got there. Something strange was going on here, but what? No time to solve the puzzle, she thought.

Her nose caught another whiff of the delicious treat Martin brought in. She marched to the front of the store with the cobbler and some plates to share with customers, and retreated to her cozy back office to hunker down to work on the NIZ grant.

Chapter 16

The morning was a whirl of activity. Stacey texted Grant to let him know that she found the NIZ proposal. "B more careful," he texted back. "That was a lot of wasted gas 4 nothing," he added. Pushing her annoyance behind her, she spent most of her time writing the grant proposal to move into the larger, more visible space downtown. It was always more work than it seemed to create a budget, a business plan and to project future sales. It was work Stacey enjoyed, and when she looked up from her computer it was closing in on noon, so she wrapped herself in her burgundy cashmere wrap, adjusted her make-up and hair a bit, climbed into her SUV and headed downtown.

She found a spot right in front of the NIZ office, walked in and delivered her grant proposal in person.

"Ms. Falesh-Gutton, so glad you are interested in moving downtown," the coordinator said to her as she explained what was in the envelope. "I watch you all the time on *You've Got To Buy That Dress!* and I'm a big fan," she added. Stacey was starting to get used to her new found celebrity and was thrilled at the impact it was having on her business. Every time she appeared on the show, new customers rolled into the store, eager to get consulted by a television star bridal consultant. More and more customers were asking for her photo, and after she was quoted in a national newspaper, a literary agent contacted her about writing a book about emerging bridal trends. She smiled at the thought of expanding the business, and was filled with a sense of pride about how well things were going for her professionally. Knowing that she built the business, and her own reputation as an expert out of sheer determination made her proud.

Remembering that it was her mother that pointed her in the direction of a career in the bridal industry made it that much more meaningful. When she realized her commitment to meet Cas for lunch, she felt a sharp pain in her stomach. Reluctantly she walked the two blocks to Casa Mia, thinking all the time how she would be firm with him and cut it off.

What am I getting into?

As she entered she could see Cas was already there, looking dapper as hell. His olive skin was holding on to its youthful appearance, and his hair was still a little damp. As she moved close to him, she noticed he smelled good, too. "You look beautiful, Stacey," he greeted her. The energy between them was undeniable. There was warmth and the connection that only comes from an old relationship. It wasn't just that Cas looked good. Stacey wasn't that shallow, but he *was* good. In her eyes he was always the model of manhood Stacey subconsciously compared every other man, too, whether she really knew them or not. Sometimes she'd scan all the heads in the pews in church in front of her and try to find another head of black, bluish thick, wavy hair and she would be reminded of Cas. She'd see a tall, thin man in a camel overcoat and think how good that coat would look on Cas. Now, with his noble single fatherhood in the aftermath of his wife's tragic accident, and his successful business, he was irresistible. And that he found her irresistible, was probably what was making him so irresistible. He loved her look, and he never stopped telling her that. He loved how shapely she was. He loved her big blue eyes. He loved how she dressed and how meticulous she was, and he told her, too. He was a man of emotion, and he was pouring his emotion on Stacey.

He leaned over, right at the table at lunch, and he kissed her on the lips. Stacey could feel her throat tighten and her eyes were getting watery. "Are you OK, Stace?" He always called her that. No one else ever did.

"Yes, of course," she tried to sound casual.

"Cas, I just don't think it is a good idea for us to see each other," she started.

Locking his smokey grey eyes with hers he said, "Let's just have a nice lunch." He was so dark complected that his 5 o'clock shadow was already appearing and it wasn't even one. There was a masculinity to him that Stacey found compelling. She forgot just *how*. "The menu looks good," he added, trying to keep it positive.

"Cas. I have feelings for you. I'm not going to deny that. But what good does it do to act on those feelings?" she asked, pleadingly. "I have a family and I don't want to mess things up," she added.

"I understand," he said.

They ordered lunch and Cas was his usual charming, self deprecating self. She remembers that he wasn't a good writer, and couldn't spell even the most common words, and she helped him with his writing coursework all throughout college. They laughed remembering how one professor was on to him, and wrote at the bottom of one of Cas's papers: "Tell your girlfriend this paper is very good." Stacey burst out laughing at the memory and a few heads turned to look. She couldn't remember the last time she enjoyed seeing someone so much.

The subject Cas excelled in was math, and he could code instinctively, without even taking a course. He described his company's slow rise to sustainability and his luck in having a tech giant approach him to buy his unique mobile app service he created a few years ago. "That, and Denise's life insurance, has made my financial life very comfortable," he said. "I want to share that comfort with someone, though. I'm lonely," he added.

Stacey could not, for the life of her, understand how a man as successful, handsome, funny, charming and dashing could still be single. She was thinking that maybe it is time to introduce Lisa to him. She wondered if she could stand to see Lisa with him. Probably not.

She tried hard to keep thinking about how sweet Grant is, and how good her life is with him and the kids. "Do you know that I used to set my TV for *You've Got To Buy That Dress!* just to catch a glimpse of you?" he mushed. "If you weren't on, I would just shut it off and wallow in my sorrow," he said.

"Cas, please," Stacey began. "Please don't talk to me like that," she added. "I'm trying to set boundaries and you are making it really hard," she said.

"Stacey, remember that dessert your mom always made? What was it called?" he asked.

"Fruit treat," Stacey said. "I haven't thought about that in years," she added. She did think about her mom's dessert, and all of the delicious food her mother effortlessly made all the time. When her mother in law brought over a baked, store bought frozen apple pie because she knew Stacey loved apple pie, all she could think of was how truly delicious her mother's homemade apple pie was. The secret is in keeping the butter cold, she remembered her mom saying. She would give anything for a slice of her mother's pie now. How did Cas know?

Cas was always so kind and deferential to her mother.

She remembers the first date they had. He showed up at the door with a dozen roses for Stacey, and another dozen for her mom. Her mother could not remember the last time a man gave her a dozen roses, maybe never, but after that night, Cas could do no wrong. Her mother used to ask Stacey to see if he wants to join them for dinner, and she would clip articles that she thought he would like and save them for him. Mrs. Falesh loved Cas, especially because she was Polish and he loved all of her Polish cooking. She could still hear him saying, "I love to come home for your good cooking, Mrs. F!" Stacey could physically feel herself falling for him all over again. He felt like family, like a long lost dead lover who has come back to life. What was she going to do? She could feel his love swallowing her up. Just the way he looked at her sent a shiver down her spine, but it was so much more than that.

He was everything she thought she was missing: a long shared history, family, someone who was truly crazy about her, excitement, romance. Stacey's mind was reeling. Cas picked up the tab for lunch, took her hand and asked her to take a walk with him.

"I cannot walk with you, Cas. People know who I am, and they know Grant too," she protested. As she said this she could see the Rotary Fountain in the distance where just a week ago, she and Grant stood on the brick they donated. A local newspaper reporter took their picture, and it appeared in a story about the revitalization of the downtown.

"Just a block," he said. "Show me where your new location will be," he asked.

"OK, just really quick," she said and she led him down Hamilton Street to 11th Street and the proposed new location.

"Wow, this is nice," he said and when he tried the door to the building, it opened. Stacey started explaining how much larger the space would be and how much more inventory they could offer. Cas took her hand and headed toward the back of the building, away from the large front window. As they slid behind some old plywood sheets, he took her in his arms, pulled her to him and kissed her passionately. She could feel herself swallowed up by his love. She kissed him again and before she knew it they were passionately making love against the wall. He was a skillful, tender lover and she could feel those old feelings coming back. With him, she was transported back to a wide-eyed, innocent girl. She knew this was a mistake, but she didn't want to stop it. For the first time in a long time, she felt young and beautiful again. Cas made her feel that way. She pulled herself together, and when she looked at her watch she realized it was almost two-thirty.

"I need to go back to the salon," she said and she kissed Cas goodbye and headed out onto Hamilton Street, toward her car, wracked with guilt, and at the same time feeling better than she had in a long time.

This has got to stop, and I'm the only one who can stop it.

Chapter 17

When she got back to Golden Day, it was almost three, and Martin looked fit to be tied when he greeted her with "Where the hell were you? You blew the interview with Brides Today magazine." Stacey had completely forgotten. "I tried to get the reporter to wait, but she said they are bumping up against the deadline. I doubt it, but maybe you can call her back and still get in."

Martin could be very dramatic, and sometimes a little gruff. It's why sometimes Chloe and Zach moaned when Stacey would invite him over. But his super intense persona was part of his success, and people had a hard time saying no to him. Martin hated to miss an opportunity to publicize the salon, and he was very forceful about following up on leads for new business. Stacey dialed the number on the card, but it went right to voicemail.

"I got caught up in the NIZ office and I toured our new space again," she said. Martin gave her stern look of disappointment and shook his head.

"You gotta keep the appointments, kid. The publicity for the new place is the key to making it a destination place," he added.

She felt terrible about missing the interview, but before she could think too much about it, her cell phone rang. It was Chloe. "Mommmmm, where ARE you? Remember, you promised to take me for boots right after school today." Chloe was waiting at her school, the last one left to be picked up. Stacey's heart started to beat out of her chest.

"Chloe, I'm sorry, I completely forgot. I'll be right there." Zach went right to track practice after school and was getting a ride home with his friend Joseph, so he was covered. Stacey remembered how Chloe asked if they could have a little "mom-daughter" time, and she felt terrible for forgetting about it. Usually, she immediately marked her calendar on her cell phone, and it kept her on track all day. She often printed out her daily schedule, and kept one at the front of the store, and one in her back office, just so nothing would be missed.

This is what happens when you allow your life to get screwed up.

"Martin, I have to run. Promised Chloe some shopping time," she said.

"Oh, don't worry about it. Just let me know when you feel like running your business again," he said sarcastically, but Stacey knew, or at least hoped that he was teasing. Nancy and Lisa were in the store, they were fine, totally covered till they close at seven, but Martin could not help but make Stacey feel badly for forgetting the meeting with Brides Today. He was always lining up good interviews and opportunities, and though he gave the magazine an interview on behalf of the salon, Stacey was the star.

Stacey jumped into her SUV and pulled a bag of chocolates out of the glove box. Totally stressed, the last thing she wanted to do was go shopping at the mall, but she was at Chloe's school in record time. Chloe stood at the curb, alone, with her head down, waiting for her. As she pulled up, she swore she caught a glimpse of Cas. That's ridiculous, she thought.

Now every man is starting to look like Cas.

She was falling deep, and needed to redirect her thinking. She just needs to set Cas straight. Let him know that this is over.

He needs to stay away. Doesn't he have a business to run in Philadelphia? I need to make an appointment with Kat.

Kat was Stacey's therapist, but Stacey usually ended up cancelling her sessions. If she saw her six times a year, that was a lot. Stacey knew she needed help sorting out the Cas issue, which was escalating her food issue, but how to find the time?

When they pulled into the mall, Chloe headed straight to Kauffmann's. They had an awesome boots department, and Chloe knew exactly what she wanted: suede, lace-up black boots with three inch heels, at least. Stacey followed behind and they both started looking for "the ones." Chloe has suddenly become a little more fussy about everything she wears. Still nothing like most girl her age, but Stacey thought it might never happen. She'd been the easy child. Not nearly as moody as Zach, she seemed to go with the flow, but lately she had become more irritated by little things, and Stacey caught her weighing herself more and staring at herself in the mirror, judging her body and asking questions about being too fat.

"Mom, what do you think of these?" she asked as she held up a pair of black, suede thigh-high boots.

"Well, they are pretty sexy," Stacey said.

"Mom, ewww, just hearing you say that is gross," Chloe said. Her phone rang, and Stacey tensed. "What's wrong, Mom?" Chloe was always so perceptive.

"Nothing, just busier than usual at the salon." She could see that Cas called. Her text went off, and she knew that he was trying to reach her. "Please call me," he texted. "Can't. With Chloe," she responded.

And this is how it starts.

As much as she didn't want to contact him, or respond to him, she was drawn to him, too. He was charming, handsome, successful and most of all, he reminded her of her parents. In a strange way, seeing him made them alive again. Like overeating those fun-size candy bars, she thought: sweet, addictive, seemingly harmless, and a way to instantly transport yourself back to childhood. But, once you start, it is hard to stop. Stacey was thinking about Cas *and* candy when Chloe spotted a pair of black leather boots, a little more practical than the other ones and tried them on. They both agreed that they looked great. And they were fifty percent off.

"Done!" Stacey exclaimed.

"Thanks, Mom," Chloe said. Stacey was happy to have this time with Chloe, and didn't just want to leave the mall, so she suggested they walk around a discount clothing shop. Because she was petite, Stacey could buy discount clothes and look good in them, if she was savvy with her selections. One of her favorite blouses, a royal blue, sleeveless, bow blouse, came from Always Young, and cost less than twenty dollars. Even Ellen from *You've Got To Buy That Dress!* asked her where she got it. Chloe and Stacey ended up in the dressing room, trying on dozens of dresses, blouses, and jeans and found a mound of clothes that they both liked. Stacey laughed when two big bags of clothes came to less than one hundred dollars.

"That was so fun, Mom, thanks," Chloe said. Stacey wanted to extend the time with Chloe. It was such a good moment and a great distraction.

"Want a coffee?" Stacey asked.

"I'd love some!" Chloe exclaimed, and they headed to the trendy coffee shop in the middle of the mall. For once, the line was less than twenty people long. "I'm getting hungry," Chloe said, so they split a pumpkin bread, Stacey making sure that Chloe ate most of it, shoving hers into her napkin, and then they headed home.

Grant would be late tonight, since he was meeting with a new employee for dinner. His company started a mentoring program, and he was assigned to a young engineer who moved from Seattle. Stacey went upstairs, changed into her "home clothes" as the kids used to call them (yoga pants and a sweatshirt) and came down to start dinner. Chloe really did look great in those new boots, so grown up. Stacey caught a glimpse of her modeling them in front of her full length mirror in her room. Zach came in and shouted "I'm starved!" He went right to the fridge looking for cheese. The three of them sat down and ate the roasted vegetable salad and margarita pizza. The meal kit came through again. In less than thirty minutes they were sitting down to a healthy meal. Stacey only ate the salad, and Zach and Chloe polished off a whole pizza between them. Grant said the meal kits were too much money and that they should stop the subscription, but Stacey really enjoyed the convenience, and it was good to be together, sitting at the kitchen table. In her mind dinner should at least take more time to eat than it did to prepare, and the meal kits made that possible.

Stacey hoped that Grant's mentoring dinner was going well. He always seemed to enjoy welcoming the new engineers to the firm and providing them with support as they got used to the area and the company. Plus, all the expenses went right to the company purchasing card. For once, neither Chloe or Zach had an evening activity, and Stacey was grateful to stay home, her mom-mobile in the garage for the night.

After roaming the mall alone for hours, Cas went home to his empty apartment, with an angry, bitter expression on his face. His tiny,one bedroom studio was only enough for one person, and he went straight to a laptop on a small table to the side of the tiny living room. He logged on and stared at images of both the old Golden Day Bridal Salon and the new downtown building. He could see who was going in and out, and then he brought up Stacey's email account. He was an IT wizard, and he was using it to his advantage to get inside of Stacey's head. He wanted to know what was going on in her life. Next he pulled up the Gutton home. He could see the outside of the house, the garage, and he could see that the garage door was down for the night. On the wall he had an old photo of Stacey and him from her high school prom, and above her photo the word Chloe was scrawled in thick black marker. He went onto a blog site and started scrolling through photos of pretty young women, scantily dressed. He typed, "I want a sweet little girl to spend my time with," and in minutes someone typed back, "Hello there, I'm Cherise." Cas spent the night sharing his fantasies, wild-eyed, angry, and alone.

Chapter 18

Back in Philadelphia, Police Chief Walt Armstrong was enjoying his retirement celebration. After forty years with the force, it was time. His wife Linda kept leaving brochures for river cruises on his nightstand, and he got the hint. He couldn't remember the last time they had a vacation. He was always on call on holidays, weekends, and even in middle of the night. He was devoted to his work, and looking at the packed room of well wishers who wanted to give him a good send off, it was clear that his career had a tremendous impact. The cafeteria at the barracks was packed, and even though the staff had wanted to host a more elaborate event at a local hotel, Walt would not hear of it.

"I don't want people to have to pay to celebrate me," he said. Instead, he got the department to start a scholarship fund for the children of slain parents. "That means more to me than anything. Over the years I've seen a lot of families suffer," he said.

He funded his going away party himself with Geno's cheesesteaks, soft pretzels and Italian ice.

His nephew Nick Delmar, heir apparent to the chief post, hugged his uncle hard. "You are everything to me, Uncle Walt. When I lost my parents, you made sure I was OK. I love you, man," he said. Both men wiped tears from their eyes. Nick's parents, Walt's brother and his wife, were victims of a terrorist attack. The terrorist, Sapor Zaiprov shouted "Allahu Akbar" as he aimed for the crowded street of innocent shoppers, driving a rented van on Broad Street and killing twelve people, including, Nick's mother and father, who died at the scene. Nick was eight years old, and Walt and his wife Linda raised him like their own, but they always kept the memory of his brother and sister in law alive.

"Is there anything specific you want me to work on, now that you are retired? Any cold cases that still keep you up at night?"

"There is only one," Walt said, without any hesitation. "The Ferraro case."

Walt didn't know if Nick knew of the case, so, always working, even at his retirement party, he found a quiet corner in the hallway, and recounted the situation: wife, suffering from mental illness, dies from a fall out of a second story window and it is ruled an accident.

"Your Aunt Linda knew Denise Ferraro from the community pool. She brought the kids to the pool almost every afternoon in the summer and she was devoted to them, overseeing their swim lessons, packing a lunch to share with them at the pool. You could see that she was a good person, and in all my years, I doubted that her fall was accidental. She had her problems, but it all seemed too convenient. A fall out of a window? The husband seemed to move on quickly after her death, and I never thought we questioned him enough," he added. I think his name was Casimir, or something like that. He was an EMT, and he knew the guys on the ambulance, so, I don't know, maybe he got a pass."

Nick could see how much the case got to him. "I've seen a lot of grieving spouses," Walt continued, "and his tears looked like crocodile to me. The whole thing seemed too neat and tidy. It has been years, and it still bothers me to no end."

"You got it, Uncle Walt. I'll reopen the case and review everything," Nick said. "But, come on, this is about you tonight. Let's celebrate." Nick stood up and gave a toast to "the best police chief Philadelphia will ever have and in my eyes, the greatest man in the world," and the room broke out into applause and tears. Walt Armstrong would be missed, but he raised Nick right, and no one in the city of Philadelphia had anything to worry about with Nick Delmar following in his footsteps.

Chapter 19

At the salon the next day, business was swift. Back to back appointments, a lunch meeting, and an early close to accommodate Bailey Grift's top secret appointment. Finally, Stacey sat down long enough to return the phone calls that had come in over a week ago. She dialed Mary Ann Redd's number, and she recognized her familiar, friendly voice.

"Stacey, thank you so much for calling me back! It is SO great to hear your voice again! I love watching you on TV. You're awesome! Did you get my message?" she asked, breathlessly.

"Yes, Mary Ann. It is so good to talk with you again, too," Stacey fibbed a little. It wasn't that she was against reconnecting, but she was just so busy, and the thought of heading to her high school reunion was not one she could feel excited about. She was touched about the award, though, and she thought that it could potentially be nice to go home again, but it also stirred up a lot of emotion for her. "I am so honored with the alumni award, that I don't know what to say," she added. Self-deprecatingly she said, "You must have not been able to connect with the real achievers in our class."

Mary Ann said that she was the unanimous choice, even though there were other impressive alumni, including a judge, a college president and an award-winning author. Stacey just felt a little embarrassed about the awkwardness of reunions even though she was being honored. Although everyone saw her as an extrovert, she found making small talk, meeting, and mingling torturous. After the initial hellos and the sharing of children's photos, then what? If she wanted to keep in touch with her high school crowd, she would already be connected to them. In the age of Facebook, it could not be easier, and after being on Facebook for years, she deactivated her account. She just didn't have the time to be posting her every move, and decided she'd put that energy into her business. Maybe a little mystery was a good thing.

Who really cares what I ate for lunch?

"This year's reunion will be at the Tooty's Cafe and Catering, and it'll include all years. We've been having trouble getting more than fifty people for our class, so we are going to open it up to a larger group. I really hope you can come, Stacey! So many people would love to see you," she added.

"Of course, Mary Ann. I'll be there. It is such an honor. I don't really know what to say," she replied, trying to be gracious. Mary Ann filled her in on all the specifics, mostly that it would be great if Grant and the kids could come. She said that the local paper had already expressed interest in writing a feature story on her, Golden Day Bridals, and her newfound TV fame. Stacey agreed to the whole thing, added the event to her calendar, and then heard her phone buzz. Mary Ann Redds "liked" the Golden Day Bridal Salon on Facebook.

I'm so glad I'm not on Facebook.

The producer from *You've Got To Buy That Dress!* called three times. Stacey was so relieved that Martin would step in for her. She knew the next few weeks would be jammed with architect meetings to finalize the new location, and even though New York is only two hours away, when you agree to appear on the show, you lose the entire day, possibly two, if the taping runs long.

She worried about not having Martin at the salon, but the publicity he would bring in for the salon would be well worth it. She thought about hiring another consultant, and made a mental note that once the move was complete that would be a top priority.

When Stacey reached Mary Ellen, the producer, she learned about a special program featuring mothers and daughters and prom dress shopping. "I know it is a little off the bridal path, but I remember your daughter Chloe from the time you brought her with you to watch the taping, and I think she'd be perfect. We are inviting three mothers and daughters to go prom dress shopping and share your experiences with our viewers," she said.

Stacey knew that Chloe would absolutely love being part of the show. Without even asking Chloe, Stacey agreed to it. She'd been feeling guilty about working so much, and this is something they could do together that was also helping business. When Stacey texted Chloe to ask her, and, as expected, Chloe texted back, "OMG, that is so cool, YESSSSS!" They would stay over in New York City one night since the taping would be two full days. Something to look forward to.

When she hung up the phone, she went to the front of the salon and hung the "Sorry We're Closed" sign. She waited for Bailey Grift's entourage to arrive. Bailey arrived, unrecognizable in no makeup, a baseball cap, blue jeans and a tee shirt, six people, including her mother and sister, in tow. She was a sweet girl, all of twenty-three, six-feet tall and waif-like in her slenderness.

This will be easy. Everything will look amazing on her.

"I want something classic, but with a little edge,

maybe even a dash of an accent color," she said quietly, her soft spoken voice in sharp contrast to her dominatrix role in her latest music video. Stacey could not believe the contrast. She seemed actually timid and shy in person. As much as she wanted to ask for an autograph, for Chloe, she resisted, and she had to agree that only two consultants from the salon would be present during the fitting. No family and friends, Bailey's rep insisted when they booked the appointment.

A body guard was staked out at the front of the store. All the designers offered custom options for clients willing to pay up to double the price of the gown, and Bailey said that would be fine. It was obvious that price was not the issue. Unlike most interactions between mother and daughter, the price of the gown would not even enter into this conversation.

There were some stunning new arrivals from Aaron Arnold, and the blush ball gown with the red sash looked like it was made for her. Stacey had done her research, and had reviewed Bailey's gown choices for the past five music award red carpet events. She seemed to favor a ball gown look, but it was clear that her mother was used to running the show. She asked for no less than twenty-two different gowns to be pulled from the racks, everything from strapless mermaid silhouettes that made her long legs look endless to princess ball gowns with sequins. The mother pulled out a notebook, making notes about how to customize each one.

Martin and Bailey's mom were poring over the Israeli designs when the body guard alerted Bailey's group that he needed to step outside to approach someone who had been looking inside the picture window the entire time that Bailey was inside. Usually it was just a nosy onlooker who may have seen the group enter, he thought, but the bodyguard wasn't taking any chances. He stepped outside, but as he walked toward the tall, slim male, he seemed to disappear into a group of people coming out of the arena from a concert. Stacey had the sick feeling that it must have been Cas. She felt that he was always watching her, and that he was just outside the door.

Another hour and a half passed, and Bailey and her group left with her choice narrowed down to two dresses, custom altered to her specifications. Bailey hardly said a full sentence during the whole time. You could see how she shot to fame before her braces were even off her teeth: her mom was the ultimate stage mother, and she took control of this situation, too, declaring: "We'd like both of them." It was not uncommon for high profile brides to purchase two gowns in the event that one of the designs inadvertently got released to the press. Or, some celebrities planned on wearing two dresses for their wedding, changing mid-way through the reception. Stacey imagined that for a celebrity, a wedding might feel like just another performance.

I wonder what it is like to be so famous.

She was sworn to complete secrecy and would never reveal the designs to the media. Stacey kept wondering how Golden Day got onto the radar of Bailey Grift and her people. The mystery was solved: "We've seen you on *You've Got To Buy That Dress!* and you are just as nice in person," said her representative as she packed up, a red head with oversized black glasses and a scarf tied on her head, old Hollywood star-style.

They seemed to trust Stacey instinctively, but that didn't prevent her manager from asking for a signature on a document guaranteeing that Golden Day, Stacey, or anyone else associated with the salon would reveal to anyone the dress style, color, designer, or even that Bailey had been in to Golden Day.

"You are free to post a photo on the wall after the wedding," the manager said. "But we don't want any media interviews at any time." Stacey would never breach the contract, but she also knew that it was likely that the media would find out that her salon provided the dress, and she would get a lot more business just from that. In a town the size of Allentown, word of these types of things usually leaked out. This was the first truly high profile client, and Stacey wanted to ensure her satisfaction, thus signaling to other celebrities that Golden Day is a discreet place for high profile brides to get the privacy they crave. One thing is certain: Bailey Grift would be a knock-out on her wedding day, and Golden Day would be the reason.

When Team Bailey Grift finally left, Stacey returned to the front of the store, feeling the pressure of the whole undertaking lifting, but before she could let down her guard, she found herself catching her breath. There was Cas, talking with Martin and Lisa. "May I help you?" Stacey asked, trying to sound casual.

"My youngest is getting ready for prom and I wondered if you also carried prom dresses," he said, all concerned parent, with a softness to his face that Staceydid not recognize. "No, just bridal dresses here," Stacey said stiffly.

"OK, thanks," he said and he turned back and winked at her as he left the store. Stacey stood there frozen. It was as though he overheard the conversation with the producers of the show and knew that Chloe would be featured on a prom show.

And what was he thinking walking in here like that?

Nancy looked lustful: "What a cutie. And I felt so bad when he started talking about why he is prom dress shopping. His wife died. Poor thing. He's been raising the children on his own. That has to be tough," she added. Lisa had a wounded expression on her face.

"Yes, he was definitely a looker, and he seemed so sweet the way he spoke of his daughter. What a sad story. I could help him wipe his tears," she added playfully. Stacey took in the scene, too numb to even speak.

She excused herself and went back to her office, closing the door behind her. She dialed Cas's number, and steeled herself.

"Don't EVER come in here again, Cas," she said harshly.

Cas said, "I just wanted to see how your salon is shaping up. It's absolutely beautiful. And Renee will need a prom dress soon. Please don't be cross with me. I know I can't ever be in your life, Stacey, so I thought maybe I could be around it, you know? I'm sorry. Let me make it up to you," he said. "Can you meet for drinks?"

The truth is she could meet for drinks. Both kids had sports practice after school, and Grant was taking the new hire for a tour of the hockey arena and a game after dinner. It was another late night for him.

"Not a good idea, Cas," she heard herself saying but she was thinking that it would be so great to see him, to touch him again.

Sensing her hesitancy, Cas said, "Listen, I'm going to the pub on the corner for a beer. I'll be there for two hours at least. If you can pop in, I'd love to see you. One drink."

It mystified Stacey how Cas seemed to just pop up all the time. She was conflicted. She thought about stopping, but instead she swiftly drove past the pub and headed straight for home. She stuffed her face with red licorice she had stashed in the glove box and spat it into an old travel mug. When she got to her garage she threw the cup right into the garbage can. She was a nervous wreck, but at least she avoided another Cas encounter.

Good girl. Any port in the storm. That licorice was so sweet.

She pulled into the garage, ran straight upstairs and threw on her "home clothes" when her cell phone rang.

"No time for an old friend, I guess," Cas said. "Getting too famous for us 'little people?'" he added. Stacey felt frightened, thinking that he must have seen Bailey Grift and her team in the salon. "And now you are just home alone. Someday the bright lights and all the offers for companionship are going to dry up, Stacey. And how will it make you feel to know that you could of had true romance, someone who really knows and loves you, but you passed it by for a man who barely notices you?"

"Cas, you are scaring me," she began. "Please, Cas. Why are you doing this now? I think I made myself clear," she added. She hung up the phone, and googled Cas Ferraro. Not too many hits. His company website and an old article about his wife's death, a short police report. She was rattled and wondered how she could get him out of her life.

She could hear Chloe and Zach coming through the door, dropped off by a neighbor whose kids go to the same school. "You know you liked it," Cas texted. Frantic, Stacey deleted the text, as if deleting his text would make Cas go away.

I don't know what I'm going to do.

For the moment, she had to put on a happy front. The public television station was airing the program on local women entrepreneurs, and her segment on building a bridal empire was airing tonight. Grant invited his parents over to watch the show and have dessert. Grant was picking up a cheesecake on his way home. Betta and Isaac showed up an hour early, bickering as usual. Something about Betta wanting to go to Deal Mart for new jeans and Isaac rushing her out of the store.

"If you made a better living, I wouldn't be shopping at Deal Mart," she walked in the door complaining. Isaac just laughed. The older he got the more he just laughed instead of confronting Betta. Stacey found the whole thing awkward as usual, but she was gracious, offered them drinks, and Betta busied herself studying the new living room furniture, suggesting a better layout and reflecting on how she could also use a new sofa.

Grant's appearance with that cheesecake could not come soon enough. Zach and Chloe bounded down the stairs when they heard him coming through the door. They filled their plates with cheesecake and whipped cream, settling in the family room to watch the public television special on Stacey, Golden Day and the impact that little Lehigh Valley was having on the national bridal industry. Stacey refused the cake, and Betta made a comment.

"I lost ten pounds," she said, "but no one ever notices," she added.

"You look good, Betta. Keep up the good work," Stacey said.

"Shhhh," Grant said and the program began.

The show opened with the perky young announcer in her form fitting royal blue dress declaring, "It used to be that for the finest wedding fashions, brides knew that New York or Philadelphia were the best options. That is until Golden Day Bridals. Stacey Falesh-Gutton and her qualified, accommodating staff have turned bridal fashions upside down in the Lehigh Valley!"

Stacey artfully dodged the question about a famous music celebrity buying her gown at Golden Day and shared what makes Golden Day unique: extreme personal service and an ever-expanding line of fashions from around the world.

The first part of the program showed the interview at Golden Day. In the second part, the television studio arranged to have a live studio audience and fashion show. Stacey remembered that when the program was recorded, the lights were so bright she could barely see the people in the audience. But sitting at home, watching the program, many of the audience members were clearly visible.

As the camera zoomed in, she could see Cas sitting in the middle of audience, smiling wickedly and leering as Chloe, one of the models, strutted across the stage in a skin tight beige lace gown.

"You're not eating, Stacey," Betta noticed. Stacey cut herself a small slice of cake while Betta declared that she rarely eats desserts. Stacey was realizing that Cas was determined to be a part of her life, and it may not be as easy a fix to turn him away as she hoped. He was starting to act as though she owed him something. But what? She realized that she needed someone to tell and there would be only one person who would listen without judgement.

Chapter 20

As soon as Stacey got to the salon the next day she asked Martin to have lunch with her.

"Sure, boss," he said right away, and then teasing Nancy and Lisa, he deadpanned, "I always knew I was her favorite child." Over lunch at the Olive Branch, Stacey told Martin everything. He was older, completely non-judgemental, more experienced, and above all, a loyal friend.

"I slept with him, Martin," she said. "I was unfaithful to my husband, and now he won't leave me alone. It is like every time I turn around, there he is. And I am a little afraid of him. What's worse, when I tell him I won't see him anymore, he seems to find a way back into my life, and I just don't know what to do." She recounted the many times Cas had just appeared, including in the television audience of the PBS program on local entrepreneurs. Martin grew serious.

Martin had a gift of an almost photographic memory, which came in handy for recognizing customers everywhere he went. It didn't matter if the wedding was last week or years ago, Martin remembered the bride, the mother of the bride, and the wedding gown. He was good. He instantly remembered Cas coming into the store, and he also remembered him from the downtown NIZ meeting. Cas's firm was hired to install and maintain IT services for every NIZ grant awardee. He remembers it for a few reasons, he thought:

"Why a Philadelphia company?" he remembered wondering as the company was announced. He also remembered him because Cas looked great when he stood up to be acknowledged. His Fermenegildo Negna suit hung on his trim frame and his hair was slicked back. Standing next to the short and fat mayor of Allentown, he looked like a movie star.

Stacey could see Martin's mind at work. "Martin, I don't know what to do," she wailed.

"Well first, I would say, stop beating yourself up. You are human. You made a mistake. We all do that. It is part of life. I could tell you've been stressed the past few weeks. I can always see it on your face," he added.

What he didn't add, kindly, is that he could see it on her body, too. Stacey's weight had been creeping up because her chewing and spitting was worse than ever. Stress always sent her into a relapse and instead of losing weight, it had made her gain weight. Stacey googled it enough times to know that most people who chew and spit don't lose weight; they gain it.

"This guy seems to be trying to get you, I don't know. He seems to want more than a "happily ever after" with you, he added. "Has he ever shown up at your house?" he asked.

"Thankfully, no. I would probably have a heart attack or faint if he did," Stacey said.

Martin was very perceptive, though and he felt that there must be more to it. "Why does he show up now?" he asked. "I'm thinking he caught a glimpse of you on the show, and wanted more," he said.

"Maybe, Martin. I mean, I you may be right. He's lonely, I guess and he knows all the right things to say. But how do I get rid of him? He supposedly lives in Philadelphia, but every time I turn around, he's here in the Lehigh Valley," she said. "I have feelings for him, but I don't want to act on them. We go back a long time, and he was very fond of my parents. He was like a member of our family. They loved him too, and were almost as heartbroken as I was when we broke up. But I love my husband, and I really want to stay married," she said.

Martin shared with her the news that Cas will be in the area on a full time basis in the coming years if the NIZ project brings the amount of business to downtown Allentown as everyone hopes.

"And you've been firm with him, right?" he asked. "You told him it has to end?"

"Yes, and I did not go to have a drink with him last night even though I wanted to," she added, with her head hung in embarrassment. Martin steadied her shaking hands with his big, warm hands. It was so good to tell someone, even if there was not an immediate solution.

They drove back to the salon in silence. As they got to the salon, Martin, who was always thinking of what to do next, was now thinking out loud: "What if I spoke with him, man to man? You know, like your big brother would do if you had one. I would set him straight and let him know how frightened you are about breaking up your marriage. Maybe he just needs a good talking-to, you know?"

It was such a kind and chivalrous gesture. It is why Martin was a true friend, like the brother Stacey never had and always wanted.

"I don't know. I wish that would take care of it, but I just don't know. There is something about him that unsettles me. Thanks for being there for me. Maybe he will just disappear," she wishfully said.

When they got into the salon, Stacey went into her office to read the newspaper and follow up on some details for the new location. She saw the article announcing that Cas's company would be responsible for all IT services. She put her head in her hands and wondered how to handle this. How this could possibly even be happening? She also wondered if she could really be the reason that Cas has shown up out of nowhere and re-entered her life.

Maybe I should just tell Grant everything.

It was good to have such loyal employees, and Martin was a true friend. He never judged her, not once.

I swear he must be family.

He tenderly held her hand, wiped her tears, and told her not to worry. She knew her secret was safe with him, and even if he didn't have a solution, he was such a comfort to her.

Thank God for Martin.

Chapter 21

The producers of *You've Got To Buy That Dress!* sent a driver for Stacey and Chloe and took them right to the studio for the first day of taping. Stacey had gotten used to the red carpet treatment, but Chloe was out of her mind with excitement, Instagramming everything. #FeelingLikeAKardashian was her hashtag. After hair and makeup, Chloe looked especially beautiful, so grown up and like Stacey did back in the day. As they posed together for a photo that Chloe shared on Facebook, Twitter and Instagram. Chloe added "Twinning with my Mom" on her Facebook post, and tagged the Golden Day Salon. It got so many "likes," and well, the resemblance *was* uncanny.

When Chloe was younger, Stacey thought she saw more of Grant in her, but now that she was a young woman, she was a mini Stacey. Stacey started to lighten her hair, but even so, when Stacey's botox was fresh, they could pass for sisters. And they were funny together. Unlike many mothers and daughters, they could joke about styles they clashed on, without any undercurrent of resentment. Stacey remembered that when her jealous ex-sister in law heard she had a girl, she said, "Watch out, girls are a real handful. Boys are easier."

But that was not Stacey's experience. Chloe was a happy baby, who grew into a determined girl, who blossomed into a goal-oriented and stunning woman, and they truly got along well. When Stacey suggested a fuschia pink dress, Chloe said, "This isn't the 90s, Mom," and brought the house down. The producers were thrilled. After the first day of rehearsals, the studio audience would be added for the second day of the live shot. Chloe was over the moon, and Stacey was trying to do her best to focus on the joy of the moment.

That evening, Stacey and Chloe had a special dinner at Richard's of Naples and took in *A Brooklyn Story* on Broadway. Stacey pinched herself. It was like the old days when she was a teenager. Her mom would bring her into New York City to audition for commercials. She never hit it big. She only got cast in one small, non-speaking role for a national hamburger chain when she was fifteen. They never stayed over, or had fancy dinners, but they walked everywhere they went in New York City and often stopped at St. Patrick's Cathedral to say a prayer. It was the closest she got to traveling as a kid, and the bus trips to the big city made a lasting impression on her. Stacey remembers clearly the one Broadway show they saw: Elizabeth Taylor starred in *The Little Foxes*.

It was the first and last Broadway show her mother ever saw, and while she enjoyed it, the fifty dollar ticket price even back then was way too much for her family. She still remembers her father saying, "shows like that are a hard item, Sweet Patootie." That was his pet name for her and it is how her dad and mom described something beyond their price range: "a hard item." They never wanted to come right out and say that they couldn't afford something.

Stacey and her sisters grew up thinking they had it as good as everyone else. And in many ways, they had it better. They may not have taken a trip to Disney World, or ate out much as other families, but their parents, older than most of their friends' parents, knew how to save money. Stacey turned to Chloe at St. Patrick's as they were on their knees, and said, "we have so much to be thankful for, Chloe. Not just the show, and all that success, but our family, our good health, the fact that we have each other, don't we?"

Chloe nodded and they were both silent, thanking God and praying. Then Stacey caught a glimpse of Cas from the corner of her eye.

Oh my God, he's watching us.

"Mom, what's wrong?" Chloe could see the look of gratitude turn to panic on Stacey's face. "Nothing, Chloe. Just some work related details. When you own your own business, it is always something," she managed.

She closed her eyes and when she opened them, and looked around again, she could not see Cas. Was it an illusion? Had she really seen him, or was she just seeing things? Reality was certainly meshing with fantasy, that is for sure. It was hard to say. She swore it was him, but there are a lot of tall, thin, well dressed men in New York. She tried to convince herself that her eyes were playing tricks on her.

On their way back to the hotel, they treated themselves to generous cones of Big Day ice cream. Stacey made a note to herself not to have any bread the next day, and to stop chewing and spitting. She didn't want to gain her weight back, and the recent stressful weeks have not been a friend to her waistline. Hovering at 137 the past week, she could not get the scale back down to 135. "Only two pounds, " she told herself, but it was the heaviest she had been since she lost the weight a few years ago, and she reminded herself not to go back.

Unlike some people who could carry some weight and still look good, if her weight went beyond 140 pounds, Stacey looked stocky and older. At less than 135, she looked youthful and petite. It was crazy that five pounds could make such a big difference, but it was true. She needed to keep the weight off. She was getting photographed more and more, and she wanted to look great, but her nerves over Cas were getting the better of her.

Her cell phone rang, and her first reaction was panic, but when she looked down at the number she realized it was Grant and she could feel the relief wash over her. "How was today?" he asked. "It was great. I think we have a little movie star on our hands. Chloe loved it."

"Mom!" Chloe exaggerated, but this experience has really brought them closer. Stacey was a cool mom in Chloe's eyes, and Stacey could see that she was thinking, *this is my role model*. So cute and so precious, Stacey thought. In another year Chloe would leave for college, and Stacey wanted to make the most of this time.

"How's Zach?" she asked Grant.

"Good, he had a meeting after school for History Day. Don't forget, it's Thursday night." Stacey had forgotten, and she was starting to feel that Zach might be feeling left out.

"I'll be there, of course," Stacey said and then marked her calendar on her phone, to be sure she would not forget. She was grateful that Grant was staying on top of things with Zach, at least he didn't forget History Day too.

With the Cas distraction, the move downtown, and the TV appearances, her schedule was getting away from her. She thought about hiring an assistant, someone who would make sure she was where she needed to be, and maybe someone who could double as a bit of a bodyguard, given the circumstances. She wished Grant could take charge or at least notice that she is stressed and make a grand gesture: send a dozen roses to their hotel room, or surprise her by coming into the city with Zach for dinner as a family. He was a good husband and father. And even more than that, he was a good person. He always thought the best of others and never gossiped. But their marriage had become so routine. It was a series of events for the children, saving money for college, and keeping up with house maintenance—nothing exciting, really memorable and certainly not anything romantic. Maybe that's what marriage is, she thought: ordinary, steady, nothing grand. She knew he would never cheat on her. Ever. They never even joked about it. On a double date with the new neighbors, Sheila and George, George joked that Sheila had a "cancer list." When he saw Stacey and Grant's confused expressions, he explained that if he died of cancer, Sheila had a whole list of men she would be interested in as a replacement for him. Stacey and Grant both agreed later that it was horrifying thought, something they'd never even consider, let alone express out loud. They had a proper and courteous relationship—maybe too proper and too courteous. There was not one extra light on in the house, and the heat was as low as it could go. Ditto for their romance.

Chapter 22

It would be hard not to get caught up in the celebrity of appearing on *You've Got To Buy That Dress!* with a five star hotel, chauffeur driven limo, fine dining, and even chocolates and champagne in the hotel room. When hair, makeup, and wardrobe appeared to make Stacey and Chloe camera ready, the look on Chloe's face was priceless. She looked as if she was going to go straight to heaven. She was snapping photos on her phone and posting them as much as she was soaking it all in.

This is what it must feel like to be president and then leave office, Stacey thought. Stacey remembered seeing a documentary on the life of the late comedian Joan Rivers, and when Joan was asked what her biggest fear is in life, she didn't say dying. She said it was an empty appointment book.

Stacey kept thinking that she and Grant will need to remind Chloe that all of this attention is temporary. Both of them would go back to their prosaic family lives in the country, and eating dinners from prepackaged boxes in no time. Chloe would head off to college, anonymous in her jeans and sweaters, just like everyone else. More than anything, Stacey hoped that this big star experience would not go to her head in a bad way or change her from the sweet, easy going girl into a diva.

But for the moment, Chloe was not thinking that this was temporary. She was convinced in her mind that it would never end, and that this was just the beginning of her worldwide fame. It wasn't just the local newspaper that was running stories. The Philadelphia Post ran a story about the mother-daughter prom dress national television exposure, and of course Chloe's school newspaper picked it up as well. The pure joy on her face was priceless. If Hollywood called tomorrow with an offer to appear on a reality show, Chloe Gutton would be ready.

And why wouldn't she be? She grew up in possibly the most celebrity saturated media age of all time. She and her friends posted numerous Instagram photos daily, positioning themselves as celebrities. In their minds, they almost were celebrities and now, Chloe had a brush with the real thing. And she was a total natural in front of the camera. When the producers lined up a teal colored satin dress, she stared into the camera, and said "Really? That dress? What am I, Madonna?" The producers could not get enough of her. The audience roared. The producers did not even need the applause sign. After the first taping they stopped using it because the audience just naturally had the inclination to clap and the applause for Chloe. Chloe Gutton, little country girl from Pennsylvania, had them in the palm of her hand.

Before all of the *You've Got To Buy That Dress!* exposure, Chloe seemed unsure of her future plans. She talked about maybe going to the local Penn State campus as an undeclared major, or even taking a year off to figure it out, maybe travel with some of the money she hoped to receive as gifts from high school graduation and her babysitting jobs, but now, her mind was made up. After high school she wanted to go to NYCU, major in broadcasting and become a television reporter. Stacey was happy that the experience was leading Chloe in an educational direction, and she even saw this experience as a way to give her a head start. Stacey smiled to herself and thought that she should try to relax and enjoy the moment. She was proud and pleased to be able to provide this experience for Chloe, and with the increased income from the show appearances and the upswing in business, affording NYCU would not be an issue.

Stacey smiled broadly and looked into the packed audience of mostly all mothers and daughters. It was thrilling. Thrilling until it became terrifying, because, from the corner of her eye, Stacey caught a gut-wrenching glimpse. Standing in the back of the room, alone and seemingly captivated by what he saw, was Cas Ferraro. A smooth talker, he must have convinced the producers that he was part of the media, though he wasn't wearing credentials and had no reason to be there. Stacey's frozen expression, upon noticing his presence, said it all. He was scaring her, stalking her, and Stacey did not know what to do. A young producer, watching from the side of the set must have noticed her expression change: "Stacey—smile. Enjoy the moment," he said.

Stacey pasted a fake grin on and stared into the camera.

The producer added, "Keep smiling, Mom! You don't want to be Melania at the inauguration now, do you? Steady with the facial expressions. This is fun, remember?"

Why does pleasure sometimes turn to pain?

Later that night, when they got back to the hotel, she called Martin from an empty conference room at the hotel. She did not want Chloe to hear or suspect a thing. She told him that she saw Cas in the audience. Standing there. Just staring like a madman. She even thought she saw him wink. He seemed to be enjoying it, or playing with her, clearly knowing that if he was hoping to freak her out, it was working. He never approached her at the end of the shooting. He never phoned later. Somehow she thought this was more ominous than when he phoned and texted. She had no idea what was going through his mind. How did he find out that this was the day of the taping? None of the press included that information.

Martin was compassionate and kind as always. He remembered a story that was featured in his Valley Monthly Magazine years back on geo-tracking. He knew that the technologies had become advanced and no one could really go anywhere undetected. What he knew is that there were ways to track Cas's steps. He had already given the little trackers to friends and family and had seen them pop up on the main website. He was pretty sure he threw one into the birthday bag for Chloe, but with all his goings on of late, with appearing on TV, meeting his new dentist friend and working double-time at the salon, he couldn't remember. And because the ones he had were so old, he wasn't even sure that they worked.

Both Stacey and Martin feared that if the police get involved, Grant would need to know. Just thinking about this gave Stacey a headache, and made her crave a whole bag of red licorice or cheddar-flavored potato chips. She was grateful to have Martin to confide in. Stacey wondered what in the world she would do without Martin.

It must have been Cas at St. Patrick's. He's here in the city, and he followed us.

Chapter 23

When Stacey got back to Golden Day Bridals after the two days of appearing on *You've Got To Buy That Dress!* the store was packed even more than usual. They added extra hours to accommodate the increased appointments and promised throngs of mothers and daughters from the area that the new downtown location would include a complete room of prom gowns. The show had not even aired, but the local Dawn Chronicle ran a front page and full lifestyle page story on Stacey, Chloe and Golden Day Bridals that hit the day she got back from the city, and customers were flowing in. Now with the Philadelphia Post running a story, there was no telling just how much attention the store would receive. Dozens of invitations to speak at local organizations were waiting for Stacey on email, and a call from a New York Press reporter on the increased cost of bridal gowns needed to be returned. Stacey and Golden Day were definitely having a moment, and Stacey was trying to stay focused on her success instead of on Cas.

With the upswing in business, Stacey hired a new part-time sales associate and even had Chloe coming in every day after school. As usual, Stacey was happy to throw herself into her work. Lisa and Nancy ran up to her when she walked in.

"How was it?" they both asked.

"Oh, it was wonderful, so exciting. I am pretty sure this is the memory that Chloe will take with her from her growing up years for the rest of her life. She was enthralled with the whole process," she said.

"Maybe you have an heir for the salon," Nancy said.

"You know what, though, Stacey, you seem really stressed."

Her staff, like a second family, seemed to sense her true emotions before Grant and the kids did.

"We know that this is just a crazy time for you and Golden Day, but it is starting to show. Stacey, we are a little worried about you,"she continued.

Stacey did pack on five pounds in the past two weeks. When she stepped on the scale and saw 140, she could feel a pit in her stomach. She had not weighed this much since she lost all the weight with Pounds Down, and her chewing and spitting was sending the scale in the wrong direction. Her glove box was filled with junk food and so was her handbag.

"Which is WHY," Nancy said, "I arranged for a little 'Women of Golden Day' Spa Pampering!" she added. Nancy had contacted the MedSpa where Stacey had been going for years for botox and other skin treatments, and booked a package for she and Stacey of a facial, massage, spa lunch, and manicure-pedicure.

"It is this Friday," Lisa added, "so we cleared your schedule. You need some R&R and Martin and I will cover the store. It is all arranged, so no backing out. Plus, it will be just in time for your high school reunion, and you have to bring it for THAT!" she added with a chuckle.

It did sound like a treat and it had been years since she indulged in a facial. It was true that she regularly paid $400 every four months for botox on her forehead and crow's feet and she had her smile lines filled in, too. She decided that when she turned forty those things just bothered her and she wanted to be happy with her appearance. It was a big improvement. A little plumping to her face and slimming to her body gave her the look of someone in her thirties, instead of forties, and she liked it that way.

She wasn't afraid of growing older, instead she truly saw it as a privilege, but she didn't have to look her age, especially in her line of work. Customers were constantly comparing their figures to hers and asking, "What size are you, and how old are you?"

It was as though being in the fashion business gave everyone the right to ask questions that are usually off limits. Grant balked at how much the botox and fillers at MedSpa cost, but with Golden Day's growing success, he really could not complain about it. Stacey was making great money, and she could certainly afford this. Besides, being on TV these days meant HDTV, and every single flaw showed. Even at 135 pounds, Stacey sometimes felt self conscious standing next to the taller women on the show, so she tried to dress to elongate her figure. At a petite 5 feet 1 inch, she needed all the length she could get. Stacey felt overwhelmed by Nancy and Lisa's concern for her, and for their thoughtfulness in booking the spa and making sure the salon was covered. "You are the best friends a woman could have, you know that, I hope," she said. "Thank you so much."

The truth is that it would be hard for Stacey to truly relax and enjoy the spa gift. Was it thoughtful? Unbelievably so, but Stacey wasn't one to just lay about, even if it was a much-needed, scheduled relaxation. She brought a stack of new style books with her and the rules and regulations for city business owners too so that even if it was a day of pampering, she could get some work done.

I really need to learn to relax.

Chapter 24

It was all hands on deck to get Golden Day Bridals downtown to its new, larger location. The illuminated sign, in gold metallic with black and red letters had a sun rising in the back of it. Golden Day Bridals would be a destination shop in downtown Allentown, and anyone who still mourned the loss of Glass's Department Store twenty years earlier could dry their tears. In the final conception of Golden Day, a cafe was added that served gourmet lunches and wedding cake for dessert, and, to Grant's delight, gourmet coffee. He and Stacey even traveled to Costa Rica to forge a relationship with a Free Trade coffee plantation that would supply the cafe with organic coffee beans. It was a completely unexpected and great trip, and it was time alone for the two of them. At first Grant balked at the cost, but Stacey assured him that it was a Golden Day business expense, so he personally paid nothing, just the right price for thrifty Grant.

Isaac and Betta stepped in to take care of the kids while they were gone, and the Golden Day Team covered at the salon. Stacey tried to push the thought out of her mind that it was actually a guilt trip—her guilt—over what happened with Cas. Seeing Grant in Costa Rica, engaged in his true passion--gourmet coffee--transformed the usual unenthused Grant into someone completely different. He would spend hours discussing roasting techniques, bag designs and methods to produce the perfect cup of coffee. He even suggested to Stacey that they travel next to

Colombia and Brazil on coffee research trips.

Stacey was seeing Grant with fresh eyes. She never saw him this truly immersed and interested in anything. This was good for Golden Day, good for Grant, and perhaps the best thing to happen to their marriage in a long time.

Grant is good where it matters most. In the heart.

Stacey's second floor windowed office was across from the second story glass window restaurant and gourmet coffee cafe, where diners would sit in front of huge glass windows onto Hamilton Street. The first floor salon, featured an immense picture window and three large showrooms, one for brides, another for bridesmaids and mothers of the brides, and the third, a prom room. The entire complex contained inventory worth more than a million dollars. It was grander than even Stacey imagined. It was more than a bridal salon, it was a bridal experience. Lining the walls on the way to the fitting rooms--Martin's idea--were poster-sized prints of iconic brides on their wedding day: Jacqueline Kennedy in Anne Lowe in 1953, Audrey Hepburn in Balmain in 1954, Ellen Degeneres and Portia deRossi in Custom Zac Posen in 2008, Beyoncé in a custom gown by her mother, Tina Knowles in 2008, Ivanka Trump in a custom Vera Wang in 2009, Chelsea Clinton, also in a custom Vera Wang in 2010, the Duchess of Cambridge, the beloved Kate, in Sarah Burton for Alexander McQueen in 2011, and her sister Pippa Middleton in Giles Deacon in 2017. From now on, with celebrities like Bailey Grift who were seeking out Golden Day Bridals, the posters of famous brides would be those who found their dream gowns at none other than Golden Day Bridals. Stacey reminded herself to be sure to add Bailey Grift's poster with permission, of course, from her representative.

A gourmet baker provided the cakes at the cafe, and the lunch selections were from a high end caterer and included the heirloom tomato and beet salad Stacey loved. Food TV already called to ask if the baker would come onto the show about wedding cakes that was being planned for fall.

The chandeliers in the showrooms were from Glass's Department Store (Martin had a contact, of course) and the whole place was just impressive and impeccable. It was indeed a golden time for Golden Day, and there seemed no end in sight for expansion and opportunity.

Next, the international market, Stacey pondered. She had been researching China and India for years, and planned trips there in the coming months to scout out fresh, new global perspectives on bridal fashions. Martin reminded her that, "Global's where it is, kid. You can get everything on the Internet." Stacey knew he was right, so striking the right balance between an in-store experience and a vibrant website would be the key to future viability. And Stacey had an incredible professor from India in college who encouraged her to visit India and explore the rich culture. The ornate clothing and home furnishings from always captivated Stacey, and she cherished a sequined pillow case depicting an elephant that her professor gave her when she graduated. "Someday you will go to India and you will buy your own mementos, so keep this and remember to reach beyond your comfort zone and get out into the world," she said. Stacey cherished that gift. It was the only one she ever received from a professor and she kept it in her office as a constant reminder that there was much more out there besides Allentown, Pennsylvania. Just thinking about what global markets could do for Golden Day and for her made Stacey truly excited about the future.

Lisa, Stacey and Martin showed up at six a.m. sharp and put in a full shift, stopping briefly for lunch and then working past dinner time. Stacey had to practically kick them out of the shop, and they were exhausted. Even though they hired a mover to place the heavy pieces, there were hundreds of boxes to open, dresses to hang by size, color, designer and price, and accessories to put into place. The new salon featured one hundred and fifty different veils alone that brides could try on. Most salons relied on photos of veils, but Golden Day wanted their brides to see themselves in the veils. Displaying them took Lisa an entire week to organize, and she was just finishing up.

"Ta da!" she announced as she hung the last veil on the display hook. "Time to go home, Lisa. The veils look incredible," Stacey added. She could feel tears welling up and she walked Martin, Nancy, and Lisa to the door.

"Moving is hard, team, and I promise not to do it again," Stacey said. "I could have never, ever pulled this off without you all." They hugged each other and surveyed their handiwork together.

"Man, it looks good," Martin said finally as they broke off their tight group hug.

"Go home. See you all tomorrow, I love you all," Stacey added.

"Bye, boss. Wow, this is incredible," Martin said.

"Good night. Love you so much!" Stacey hollered after them.

"Back at ya, kid," Martin yelled back and they disappeared down Hamilton Street toward the parking garage.

Stacey was thinking how she could never, ever have built this bridal empire without a staff like that. She couldn't also help but to think that her mom had something to do with it.

She put Martin in my life, that I know.

She went back to continue to set up her office. Grant knew that she may not even get home till ten, and he wanted to come and pitch in with the setup of everything, but Stacey was just happy he could cover the kids. His parents were back in Florida, so it was just the two of them again. Chloe had cheerleading camp, and Zach was struggling with his math homework. "Just cover those two things, and make the dinner in the fridge," she said. Grant was starting to like the boxed dinner kits after all.

Stacey had gotten into the habit of watching the national news on her laptop, and she realized that it would be a nice distraction to watch her favorite national cable channel, so she put it on and began to organize her new, spacious office. She had a wall of bookcases constructed on one side to hold books and mementos. It was certainly an upgrade from her previous, cramped space that doubled as both her office and overflow veil storage room.

She could see a photo of her local congressman on the screen, and it caught her attention. She liked Charlie Foment so much that she worked on his last three campaigns, standing in front of the voting station on Election Day. Charlie was a good guy. A solid family man and friendly, too. He once joined she and Grant for an impromptu dinner after bumping into each other on Hamilton Street, and he always returned calls from constituents. She turned up the volume. The announcer, with a surprised and disappointed look on her face said, "Popular Pennsylvania Congressman Charlie Foment is stepping down after sixteen years in office. Several female staffers have come forward with alleged sexual assault charges. Foment was often mentioned as a possible presidential hopeful." Stacey stared at the computer monitor in disbelief.

No, not Charlie? Is anyone who they appear to be?

Stacey, still reeling in disbelief over the Charlie Foment story, began hanging a couple of framed media articles on the walls of her office when he simply appeared at her office door.

"Your personal IT Service," said Cas. "It comes with your NIZ proposal approval, and I'm here to make certain that Golden Day has the finest internet service, or any other service you might need," he added with a devilish grin. "You look beautiful, Stace."

Stacey's mouth went dry. She realized that the front door was still open, and the Cas had just walked in. She knew she was shaking. He genuinely frightened her, but he also tempted her.

She managed to try to keep it all business, "I know you got the contract for all the NIZ properties, Cas, but I don't think it's a good idea for you to be here," she said. "And I need to get going. It's late," she added.

Ignoring her, he looked around and said, "this place is amazing, Stace. You must be so thrilled."

"Yes, it looks great," she said. "My team is amazing," she added. "Cas, I'm uncomfortable with you here, and I think I've made that clear," she went on.

"Really? Uncomfortable, are you? The last time we were together you seemed very comfortable. Stace. I miss you. I want to be part of your life," he added.

Stacey was slightly frightened by him, but she was also a little turned on by how frightened she was. It was Casimer Ferraro after all, a very old friend, from her old town. How scary could he really be she tried to rationalize in her mind. The song by Dolly Parton was playing in her mind, "Here you come again. Just when I'd begun to get myself together. He walks right in the door, like he'd done before.....Looking better than anybody has a right to." But she re-focused herself and tried to reason with him.

"Cas, I won't deny we have history. And I do care for you." It didn't help that his massive gray eyes had a sadness to them. "But too much time has passed," she continued. My life is different now," she was trying to reason with him, but the sadness in his eyes were turning to anger. She did not recognize that look. Stacey was starting to get scared. It was just her and Cas, and Cas was starting to frighten her. She was thinking that just a few months ago, her life was so different. It might have been stressful, but re-meeting Cas was stress at a whole new level. She had to keep her feelings for him at bay because there was something about him that was different than the Cas she knew from high school and college.

Should I tell Grant? Call the police? Would Cas just back off?

"Cas, what do you want from me?" she asked.

"I want you, Stace. You know you love me. You know I'm alone," he sounded desperate.

"That's what I can't figure out," Stacey said. "Why are you alone? You are handsome, successful," she was trying to flatter him. "You've done everything right, Cas," she added. "Your parents must be so proud of you," she continued.

"Stop patronizing me. I never even see my parents. My brother was always their favorite. It must be nice to have everything. A family, fame, respect, a successful business. What do I really have, Stace?" Stacey was starting to feel threatened, but she thought she could reason with Cas.

"What do you mean, Cas? What are you even talking about? You have a great life, a life most people would envy. Your children are beautiful. Your business is thriving. I see how other women look at you. You just need the right one," she added, which was precisely the wrong thing to say.

"*You* are that woman. Come here," he said, and he pulled her toward him. The whites of her eyes getting bigger as she tried to reach for her phone to dial Martin, who would probably figure out that something is wrong. She tried to stall.

"I have a lot of work to do here, Cas, and Grant will be coming any minute to help me," she lied.

"Really, little Grant is on his way to save the day, huh?" he was being sarcastic, but he was also walking down the circular stairs, toward the door. "Would he really make the trip all the way into town with gas prices so high?" he laughed at his own joke. But then he grew serious. As he continued to make his way out, he shouted behind him as Stacey stood at the top of the circular staircase. She thought it would be better not to follow him down. "You can't push me away forever, Stace. I'll be back," he exploded as he left, angry and sweating, slamming the door so hard behind him the "Be back soon" sign plunged to the floor, ironically. Stacey waited until he was out, ran quickly down the steps, toward the door, bolting it shut, and closing the window curtains.

Her heart was beating seemingly out of her chest when she called Grant and begged.

"Grant, could you pick me up from the new salon?" Stacey asked.

"What's wrong? You OK?" he asked.

"Just got spooked. There were some people lurking around outside and they creeped me out," she lied.

"But your SUV is downtown. How will you get it home?' he asked. She hated how, even in times of complete crisis, he was always so practical, pointing out that leaving her car there could be a risk, or a waste of gas, when it was her own life she was worrying about. Maybe she should lean on her sisters more. Her sister Teri was a prison warden who had served two tours of duty in Iraq. She never liked Cas, and Stacey was sure she would scare him off if she told her what has been going on. Seeing Stacey wide-eyed after a tour of her prison, Teri, said, "What, a little spooked, sis? Just remember, we are all one stupid act away from a life behind bars." That really got to Stacey, but she knew Teri was right.

Good people do bad things. And bad people do good things, too.

And her other sister Julie was also a true friend. She'd listen, not judge, and she would try to find a solution.

I'm from good people. And blood is definitely thicker than water.

As she was calming herself and pondering her good sisters and her late, great parents, Grant pulled right up to the door. She could see the steam coming from his recycled coffee cup, and he could see she was shaking. Surprisingly, he said,"We can worry about your SUV tomorrow. I'll bring you to work."

Stacey got into his car, thinking that given Grant's magnanimous offer, she must have really looked a mess."I guess I just need to get used to this city location. It's got lots of activity outside," she said. From the corner of her eye she could see Cas watching. He was sitting in the Starbucks across the street with a dead stare on her salon. He waved as she got into the van.

Yes, he is scary, and he is scaring me.

Maybe it was time to tell Grant everything, she thought as he turned off the music on his radio and turned to her. "I told you downtown would be different," he said.

She hated when he went into "told you so" mode. When they got home, Stacey hugged Chloe and Zach tight and, as she made lunches for tomorrow she thought about how much she has and how much she loves her family. She was glad it would be Friday and that the weekend would be here. There was still a lot to do to get the salon set up, but tomorrow was Spa Day for her and Nancy, and she was trying to look forward to it.

Chapter 25

As promised, Grant took Stacey downtown to pick up her SUV, and, though there was no need for her to do anything at the salon, she could not resist going into Golden Day before she met Nancy at the MedSpa. Lisa and Martin were already there and the coffee from the cafe was wafting through the air.

"Hey, what are you doing here?" Martin asked. "It is your day to get pampered and gorgeous." Easily able to see the top of her head just by looking down, he said, "Time for a root touch up and some new highlights too, just saying," he added.

Martin was always suggesting little ways Stacey could improve her look or adopt a new trend to her advantage. Coming from any other man it would be so weird and maybe even over the line, but not from Martin. His intentions were pure sugar, and he often had a good idea about what would improve her appearance even before she did.

"You're right, I know--thank you Martin," she said a bit annoyed that he was so spot on. "I just had to peek in and make sure the dresses from New York were delivered," she said.

"No, they won't be here till eleven, and I think you know that. Don't you trust us?" Lisa teased.

"I do, I do, but with all this work to do I feel selfish getting all pampered," she said.

Martin and Lisa each took one of her hand, walked her to the door and said, "Bye -- we've got this. Try to enjoy yourself today," Lisa added.

Martin called after her, "Oh, and if you need good contacts in China, I'm making a list for you."

Stacey marveled at Martin's connections. They weren't just local, they were international. "Well, you better come with me to China, Martin," Stacey said. She did not like to travel alone, and annoying and forceful as he could be sometimes, Martin would be the ideal travel companion.

Once he met someone, that was a contact for life and he would connect the dots to make connections for her all the time. She recorded a note into her phone to remember to speak to him about that.

As she drove, listening to news on the radio, she shook her head in disbelief and disgust as another famous man was accused of sexual harassment. It was her favorite TV host, William Dazey. He seemed like such a straight-up guy. She absolutely loved his low-key television program. He always seemed first to interview a famous celebrity in the news, and he did it with such nuanced thoughtfulness. In the previous weeks high profile men, one after another were outed for their mistreatment of women. First it was a congressman, then a few well-known television and movie stars. Soon to be released films were put on hold, and television series cancelled.

And now William Dazey fired from the network. An intern claimed he slipped his hand under her skirt. She also said he groped her thirteen year old sister who was visiting her on the set by grabbing her breast and asking if they would both like to visit his hotel room after the show. His emails revealed that thinking about young women—no girls—many who were under eighteen, seemed to be his after-work hobby. He had written about "a delectable young actress whose breasts stood at attention," and "only fourteen, just getting to the sweetest years." Once these men are outed, they all offer the same generic apology. Something along the lines of "If any of my comments or actions have indeed been unwelcome or if I have conducted myself in anyway that has caused any individual discomfort, or embarrassment, I am sincerely sorry." They all sounded like disingenuous idiots to Stacey who wondered if any man was truly decent inside.

You are only sincerely sorry you got caught. How disgusting. And I admired him. You just blew your obituary!

Just a few weeks ago, she finished reading William Dazey's latest book, *Doing Good to be Great.* Now his career, and, essentially his life, are up in smoke. She tried to push it out of her mind, and, as she pulled into the MedSpa parking lot, she was hoping that a day at the spa would make the stress leave her body. Now, if she could only rest her mind, too.

The team went through a lot a work to help me relax. I have got to give it my all.

Judy was a master aesthetician, and even though Stacey never spent a whole day at the spa, because it seemed like too much hassle to get coverage for work or the kids, she tried to find the time to indulge in monthly massages. Spa, an acronym of the Latin phrase Solus Per Aqua, or "health from water," really delivered on its promise.

Upon entering, the fountain in the lobby set the tone for her experience. If there was one time in her entire life that she needed this indulgence, this was it. A good facial, a full body massage, a mani-pedi...ahhhh, it would all be so relaxing. Nancy was already there, and Stacey hugged and thanked her for doing this.

They started with massages. Stacey went with a deep tissue massage and she could feel the tension leaving her body. The first time Stacey received a massage, she could not understand why people even get massages. She absolutely hated it. The feeling of some strange man putting his hands on her while she lie naked under a towel felt terrifying. That was twenty years ago, when she had very little, at least compared to now, to be stressed about. She vowed never to get a massage again.

But since then, she had seen chain massage parlors pop up and her curiosity was piqued. She went into Massage Delight one day and asked for "the most popular massage" and said that she preferred a female masseuse. Thirty minutes later she emerged feeling like a new woman. The experience was completely different than her first spa encounter. For one, she had a female masseuse, which made her feel less exposed. She also kept her underwear on. The place was quiet, spotless, and unpretentious.

She started buying monthly massage packages, and she found that the experience helped her with emotional eating. It didn't completely stop her chewing and spitting problem, but if she was more relaxed overall, she found herself less likely to think about sugary food and thus, less likely to chew and spit. The massage membership did make her feel more relaxed in general, but it had been months since she had gotten in for her monthly massage, and between the new salon and Cas, she had not made the time like she had been.

Though Cas had escalated her eating disorder, even before her reintroduction to Cas, she was feeling very tight and enormously stressed. He was a problem, but he wasn't the whole problem. She knew that she needed to deal with the real issues: her ongoing bereavement for her parents and her constant feeling that she isn't measuring up at home or at work. She let herself think of these things as Judy dug deep into her skin and made her feel completely at ease. When her massage was finished, she had a facial alongside Nancy, and then they both got manicures and pedicures. It took almost the whole day, and Stacey managed to stay off her phone for most of it, calling into Golden Day Bridals only once.

It was three in the afternoon when Darcy from MedSpa said she could squeeze her in for a root touch up and highlights, and Stacey decided to go for it. "Martin will be pleased," she chuckled to herself. Grant on the other hand never noticed when she had her hair done, even if she changed it quite a lot. Once she had two inches cut off, had layers put in and lightened it from brown to practically bright blonde, and he never said a word. Grant has started to cut his hair really short, and Stacey found it unattractive. He had a thick head of black straight hair when she met him, but now it was mostly grey, and he had it buzzed cut every three to four weeks. She preferred men with styled hair. The gray did not bother her, but the baldy look did. No matter how many times she suggested he grow it out a bit, he always came home with the same buzz cut. Stacey tried to convince Grant to grow his hair out reasoning with him that most men his age don't even have hair--he ought to flaunt it a little--but he never would.

Aging is not for sissies.

The truth is, she was never as physically attracted to Grant as she was to Cas. She tried to help Grant with his grooming and clothing choices, but he sometimes looked like an aging school boy with his ill-fitting, budget clothes. Small in stature, men's clothing usually overwhelmed him, his pant cuffs fraying from dragging on the pavement. When it came to dressing for success, Cas was just "into it" and Grant wasn't.

Cas does look so damn good.

"Earth to Stacey," Nancy said. "I'm glad this has distracted you." Nancy headed home adding, "We should do this more often, my friend. It is just what the doctor ordered."

Stacey hugged her employee and close friend, thinking that maybe she ought to confide in her what has been happening. She was distracted all right, but not in a good way. What should be a wonderful time in her life, newfound fame, wealth, and her healthy family growing up, has become a frantic, doubtful time. She loved Grant, but she could not deny her feelings for Cas, even if some of them have been turning to fear. She wondered if she had loved Grant more, or felt more attracted to him if she would have been able to resist Cas.

Some things in life we will never know.

Stacey pushed her thoughts of Cas aside and settled into the salon chair for her hair styling, deep conditioning treatment and blow out. She brought the Sunday paper with her, even though it was days old, and pored over the obituaries with intensity.

"David Richard Rinse passed away surrounded by his family at home in Easton on Wednesday, November 12th. Dave was born in Allentown to Samuel G. Rinse and Rebecca S. (Matthews) Rinse, both of whom preceded him in death. Dave was proud of his long service in the U.S. Air Force Reserve and he stayed in touch with many of his USAF colleagues and counted them among his dearest friends."

She moved onto Jayne Seyfried, 65, who "enjoyed gardening and was a proud steward of a Little Free Library," and onward to Gerald "Jerry" Maston, 71 of Macungie who was an avid NASCAR and Eagles Fan. Stacey liked reading more about the passions of the deceased, than the professions. Rarely were the two combined, she reflected.

When the whir of the hair dryer finally stopped, and her hair was blown out, she looked positively lovely and a little edgy. The stylist cut the back a little shorter, which was a very flattering look on Stacey's broad face, and she was pleased when the stylist spun the chair around to give her the 360 look at her new and improved image.

Stacey finally pulled out her phone a let herself scroll through her messages. She noticed a call from the producers of *You've Got To Buy That Dress!* as well as several other texts and voicemails. She listened to the voicemail from the producer. She wasn't just a proud mama; the producers want to feature Chloe on billboards, social media, and in at least two more prom related episodes. Chloe would be thrilled, and the money from the show would be substantial enough to pay for her first semester of college.

And the double benefit of appearing on the show was that business at the salon would increase. Stacey thought she'd wait to tell Chloe in person as soon as she got home. On the one hand, she was thrilled for Chloe, but in the back of her motherly mind she wanted to be sure that Chloe could keep up with her academics. She worried that so much exposure would open her up to jealousy from her classmates at school, and worse, untoward interest from older men. Chloe's academics were strong.

Though Zach teased her endlessly about being in remedial algebra, the truth is that math was one of Chloe's strongest subjects. She was in a math tutoring program, not remedial math, and that was only because she breezed through every math course her school offered. Math was easy. The thought of creepy men leering at Chloe unnerved Stacey. That was hard.

I'm going to have to get her a bodyguard.

She stepped outside and as she moved toward her SUV, she kept looking over her shoulder. Cas had made her nervous and self conscious about every step she took. She opened the SUV, got inside and drove away, still glancing in the rear view mirror. She was not even half a mile away when her cell rang.

"Do you feel all pampered and fresh? I wish you were getting dolled up for me," Cas said.

"Cas," Stacey said, "you really need to stop calling me."

"Can't I see you again, Stacey? I miss you," he pleaded.

"Why are you doing this, Cas?" she asked.

"Because I want to be close to you, Stacey. I want to know your children. I want them to call me Uncle Cas. I'm your family, Stace. I want to be someone you call when you need help," he added.

"Cas, that's not possible," Stacey said.

"It could be, Stace, and you know it. You are holding the cards here. Let me in," he pleaded. "In your heart you know your marriage is not what makes you happy. Your little husband, going around shutting off the lights and turning down the heat all the time. Is that how you want to spend the rest of your life?"

Stacey's mind was racing and she was wondering who could have even told him these things? Yes, Grant was painfully thrifty, but did anyone ever leave a marriage because of it? What does she do? File for divorce and instead of "irreconcilable differences" say that the house was too cold or hot? Besides, she loved her husband, and she was starting to realize that Grant was more nuanced than she ever gave him credit for. She was trying to think how Cas could have this inside information about her marriage and family life and wondered if Cas could be listening to her conversations. She had to wonder: is he spying on her family?

"I can't, Cas, and I have to go. I'm almost home," she lied. She had another fifteen minutes of driving.

"No you're not," he said. She got a chill down her spine as she looking in her rearview mirror to see if he was following her. Her next thought was to change her cell phone number, but what a pain that would be. She had truly been thinking to come clean with Grant, tell him everything, and then go to the police. She knew, however, that that would be the true test of her marriage.

He must be following and watching me.

"Please leave me alone, Cas. You could have any woman, why me? I'm married. Please," she added and the phone went dead. The entire day of self care and pampering seemed a complete waste of time and money and the stress that slowly left her as she relaxed at the MedSpa, was back in seconds. Stacey's first instinct was to eat, but she had nothing in the car, and she just wanted to go home to Grant and the kids. She drove fast now, remembering that there were powdered sugared donuts in the freezer that Betta brought, left over from breakfast when Betta and Isaac came. Isaac loved his mini donuts.

If I call the police right now, my life is going to fall apart completely.

Chapter 26

Stacey gave Grant a knowing and grateful glance as they pulled up to Tooty's Cafe and Catering for her high school reunion. He definitely didn't want to go. Stacey wasn't really feeling like going either with Cas stalking her and the salon demanding every second of her time, but she always kept her promises. Zach and Chloe were not into it either, even though they were proud of her honor, and they usually liked seeing where she grew up, especially since they visited their aunts only a few times a year. So there they were -- none of them thrilled about it but all of them in the car ready to put on their game faces nonetheless. Stacey wanted a closer relationship with her sisters, but it always seemed like their schedules were out of sync. She thought that maybe, if the reunion wrapped up early, they would stop by and say hello to Julie on their way back to Allentown. But Larry Brunish invited everyone to "keep the party going" at a nearby bar where he and his band Funny Papers would be playing till way past midnight. Stacey initially said "no way" with a major eye bug out to Grant about the after party, especially with the kids, but Larry was so warm when he ran up to the whole family as they walked into the reunion, that she was starting to feel like squeezing out of it would be difficult.

Wow, this reunion thing was really happening. But why am I being honored?

She was starting to feel a little embarrassed about the whole thing. She had the master chef at The Golden

Day Cafe make a wedding cake-like high school reunion cake in gold and white fondant with "Vikings Forever" emblazoned on the top. It was her donation to the reunion, because she had a feeling Mary Ann was paying for a lot of things right out of her pocket, and that just wasn't right. The cake looked amazing, and everyone was oohing and ahhing over it as the wait staff from the restaurant carried it in.

In moments, Stacey was transported back to high school. People had not changed that much, really. OK, most people put on weight, some a lot of it, but if you looked past that, everyone was pretty much still like their high school selves, just older. Larry Brunish looked great. What an admirable story. Talk about staying true to yourself. He graduated with honors from Penn State with a degree in electrical engineering, but except for his over-the-top holiday light displays, he never used his degree. Instead, he followed his heart and kept up his music. He makes a living with Funny Papers, playing any venue that will hire him, even sponsoring cruise concerts. And he was so nice. His wife came over to say hello.

Stacey liked these people. She felt at home here. These were her roots, and though she could easily step into the big time with the best of them, this is where her heart has always been.

Lesley Masters stopped and looked at Chloe and said "You KNOW she's your twin, right? Oh my gosh, she's gorgeous." Chloe's face turned bright red, but she did look especially stunning for the reunion. She was wearing the designer dress Stacey bought her from her appearance on *You've Got To Buy That Dress!* The producers selected about a half dozen clothes and when the shoot ended, they were able to buy whatever they wanted at a ridiculous discount.

It was a cream Gucci halter dress and Chloe was rocking it. Lesley still looked good. A tall blond with a sophisticated air, Stacey tried to be friendly toward her in high school, but Stacey's last encounter with her was one of the worst in her high school memories.

Almost six feet tall, she pushed Stacey up against the lockers when she heard that she wanted to join the debate team. Lesley was the star of debate, and she did not want the competition. Stacey backed off, focusing her energies into the fashion shows and drama productions.

She was surprised by Lesley's over the top friendliness at the reunion, but the bar had been open for two hours, and well, time, and a little wine, has a way of erasing bad memories. She remembered that when she told Sister Carlanita about the locker bullying incident, Sister Carlanita simply said, "Pray for her." The Bishop Frances remedy for everything. Maybe praying could provide welcome solace for the stress she'd been under and she wanted to get the family to go to church more often.

More regular church attendance. Add it to the list.

Once Chloe and Zach got their sacraments, it was hard to get them piled into the SUV on the weekend for the thirty minute trip to mass, and their attendance had become sporadic. She noticed that one of the alumni, who had become a priest, would be at the event, making an invocation. She didn't know him from his name, but thought maybe she would recognize his face.

Dear Father: bring on the prayers.

Tooty's was charming, if humble, and Stacey could see why Mary Ann chose it. It had a large open ballroom and a bar, a requisite for these types of things, especially in her hometown where bars were outnumbered only by ethnic churches. And there really was a Tooty. Stacey remembers being in school with his daughter Maria. While many of the churches had closed, it seemed that the bar business was a robust as ever, and she could see Tooty himself serving up the drinks.

Grant, despite his thriftiness, could be a big snob. Stacey could see he had his "When are we leaving?" snoot on his face, especially after he scanned the sparse selection of appetizers, which consisted mostly of crackers and cheap cheese. Grant grew up on Long Island, and Stacey's humble hometown was a place he'd rather avoid. She'd had hoped that he would turn into Mr. Social, which he often did on outings where there were a lot of strangers, but he seemed in a particularly introverted mood that night, and it was stressing Stacey out even more.

When he was moody, he picked on the kids. He was already telling Zach not to wipe his mouth with his shirt, to sit up straight and not to eat so many crackers. It was going to be a long night at Tooty's Cafe.

Lesley, who seemed to want to be best friends with Stacey was back, and this time she leaned in and in a whisper asked Stacey, "What ever happened to Casimir Ferraro?" Stacey did her best to act casual.

"How should I know?" said Stacey overly loud and nonchalant and she gestured "who knows" with her hands in the air. But what she was feeling was a sharp pain in her stomach, an oncoming headache, so she plastered on a huge fake smile and walked over to the bar.

Lesley looked up toward the door and said, "Well, I guess we are about to find out," as Cas, "looking better than anyone has a right to" walked in to the reunion, alone.

"I wonder if Larry's band plays any Dolly Parton?" Stacey deadpanned to Lesley, who asked "what?" as if her hearing aid just malfunctioned.

Is this for real?

Stacey wanted to gather up her little family and leave, but before she could think of anything else, including Cas's presence, she could feel a strong squeeze.

"You look great!" Susan Cain hugged Stacey. Susan was always nice. She looked exactly like she did in high school. In high school, she had the maturity and appearance of a thirty year old woman, and now, in her early forties, she had finally caught up with herself. She was very warm, calm, serene. It was truly good to see her. She was telling Stacey that she and her husband lived in Harrisburg, she worked part time as a paralegal, they had three kids, the youngest was fourteen.

But Stacey's mind was racing because of Cas, who from the corner of her eye, she could see was already holding a drink and looking like he was relishing every moment. Stacey started to wonder if Grant would even recognize him. It had been so many years, and they had only met once at a restaurant, when they were both having dinner shortly after they broke up. Cas had been in town to visit his parents and she and Grant decided to have Italian food. She remembers feeling sick to her stomach and choked up then and she was feeling that same feeling now. He was with Denise and she looked so polished and professional in her tight capri pants and high red pumps with matching purse.

Stacey contemplated the impossible for a moment—could she just leave—maybe say that she is sick? She certainly felt sick. Zach and Chloe were bored out of their minds. There were no other children, because they were only invited to see their mom win the alumni award.

We'll leave a few minutes after the award and dinner.

What seemed like an eternity passed. Grant was still

snoot faced, drinking his subpar beer from a local brewery and not even eating the few appetizers, especially since the only addition to the appetizer buffet looked like a Jello mold. He had complained that he was starved as he was driving and had hoped for some good food. Mary Ann's husband had attached himself to Grant for some reason and was talking non-stop. Stacey overheard part of the conversation and thought that Grant must be out of his mind with agitation over having to spend his night like this. She could hear Rob Redd say, "I'm sorry my oldest boy had to do time," and Stacey winced at the thought of what Grant must be thinking.

Stacey glanced at the program. It looked straightforward enough: Welcome, Meet and Mingle, Invocation, Toasts, Dinner, Awards, Dancing and the After Party. Stacey just wished Mary Ann would get the party started. Stacey wondered who was the emcee anyway? Mary Ann came over to Stacey, hugged her, thanked her effusively for the cake, and pinned a special alumni gold and white ribbon on her. All the name tags included a photo of the students from the yearbook the year they graduated.

Zach teased Chloe, "your face is on Mom's name tag."

"Shut up, Zach," she said.

"Kids," Grant chimed in, "behave yourselves. This is Mom's big night, so be nice for her sake." Stacey appreciated that and the kids did settle down.

Thankfully, Mary Ann moved to the microphone. "Hello Everyone. Wow, a nice big group! I'm so glad you could come," she said. "We may all lead different lives but we are, to which everyone instinctively chimed in Vikings Forever! To get us started this evening, Father Mark Franchensky will lead us in prayer.

Solemnly he intoned, "Dear Heavenly Lord, thank you

for this time tonight to reflect on who we are and where we have come from. We are grateful for your love and your guidance. And for our classmates who have gone home to you, we pray for them and for their families."

Stacey thought about the large number of classmates from her class who were already deceased. That always shook her to the core. Lori, a popular cheerleader, died in an auto accident in Florida while she was in college, just a year after high school. And Ellen, smart Ellen. She just died recently of breast cancer. Another classmate in a fire. One of a heart attack. Photos of the deceased classmates were framed and set among lit candles in the reception room. It was a thoughtful remembrance, but also a stark reminded of how short life is and how we need to make the most of everything. "In the name of the Father, Son and the Holy Spirit, Amen." Stacey remembered Mark, a couple years ahead, who had been friends with Cas. She could feel Cas's eyes on her.

A prayer is an apropos way to begin the evening.

Chapter 27

The reunion seemed like the longest night of Stacey's life. As she was considering how much longer it might go on, she was checking off the evening's events: Welcome, Check! Meet and Mingle, Check! Invocation, Check! By her calculation, they just needed the toasts, dinner, awards, dancing and the after party.

Gratefully, Cas was sitting clear across the room, at Father Franchesky's table and she could not even see him where she was sitting with her family. Mary Ann went back up to the microphone. "I'd like to begin with a toast to everyone." Everyone had a small plastic champagne glass with something sparkling in it. Grant made a smug comment that "The Dollar Store" was making a big appearance that night. Stacey had a pet peeve about drinking from paper or plastic cups. She hated it, but she held her plastic champagne cup up with the best of them.

Mary Ann continued: "To the good old days, when we weren't so good, because we weren't so old. To our health, that we may drink with one another again in ten years time, and a few in between. Here's to Vikings forever, that we are here, to those who are not here, and to the rest of us everywhere! To Bishop Frances, friends forever! Let's lift our glasses from the table!"

Hear, hear, Stacey thought. Mary Ann's husband got up and took the mic. He seemed to have more than a few too many already.

"Nice job, babe! He grabbed her butt. "Doesn't she

look hot in this black mini dress?" he asked. Everyone clapped. A few people whistled. It was getting rowdy here tonight, Stacey thought. Mary Ann went back to the mic and asked if anyone else wanted to make a toast.

Tammy Trill stood up. A painfully shy girl in high school, she had not changed in appearance almost at all. Very thin, her curly hair styled in a natural look, a bit like a mop on the top of her head, she walked up to the microphone. "It is so nice to see everyone," she said. "I especially want to thank Mary Ann who did all of this for us," she said.

Again, everyone clapped. Mary Ann was enjoying the recognition, but she truly had worked hard. So many details and if it wasn't for her, there would be no reunion. "Cheers everyone," Tammy added. Short and sweet, just like Tammy.

"Any other toasts?" Mary Ann asked. The room was quiet, and the servers were coming around with the chicken cordon bleu, potatoes and green beans.

"I hope there is something vegetarian for us," Stacey whispered to Chloe. Grant's face was growing longer by the seconds and the dinner offering was not going to improve things. Mary Ann walked over to Stacey, "I had the chef prepare pasta prima vera for your family and the few other vegetarians here tonight," she said. "I hope that will be OK."

"That's perfect," Stacey said, relieved, and it really was. They all loved pasta and vegetables, and Grant could definitely use some food in him. The food was delicious and the staff at Tooty's began cutting the gorgeous cake that Stacey brought. It was welcomed by everyone and Grant even said the coffee was "not that bad," which really meant it was pretty good.

After dessert there was more mingling. Stacey was staying with her family at the table, which she thought was a good strategy for avoiding Cas, but if she moved for a moment, even to throw something out or to stand up to straighten her dress, she could see Cas watching her with a wicked look in his eye.

He is enjoying this. He thinks it's funny.

Chapter 28

Back in Philadelphia, Walt Armstrong was packing up his office when his nephew, Nick Delmar, stopped by to help.

"How do you feel, Uncle Walt? You are really packing up, huh?" Nick asked.

"Yeah, feels like yesterday I took this job," he said. "

And I don't think you cleaned out your desk since then," Nick added, holding up a picture of himself in Fourth grade. Walt laughed.

Nick knew that Walt's shoes could never really be filled at the department. He was from the greatest generation. World War II Veteran, went to college on the GI bill, and had been married to Linda for almost fifty years. They were great people, and Nick felt beyond fortunate to have his uncle as a father figure and mentor.

"Any luck looking into the Ferraro case?" Walt asked. He never embraced the new forensic based technology and instead investigated suspected murder cases on instinct. He let the younger officers delve into the new technology. He hoped that Nick would take the Ferraro case in that direction.

"I was just going to bring that up, Uncle Walt," he said.

This past month Nick had spent hours in the old Ferraro neighborhood, blending in at the bus stop, asking around subtly about the family, making contact with those who knew the family. With four children, there were many people who knew the kids, Denise, and Cas. Many of them seemed to want to get things off their chest. The death of Denise had been five years ago. Cas moved out with the younger two children, Clark and Renee, a couple years ago, relocating in center city Philadelphia. Clark had since moved out on his own, but most of the neighbors were still living around the old Ferraro neighborhood. Nick spoke to the new owners of the house, just to see if anything was left inside the house, or if they had heard anything about the former owners. It could be hard to sell a house where someone had died, but the happy-go-lucky guy who answered the door of the former Ferraro home shrugged it off and added, "You gotta die somewhere."

The Ferraros seemed to leave no trace of their former life behind in the vinyl-and faux brick sided two story home, that was an exact match, except for the color scheme, of the six homes perfectly spaced apart in the tidy cul-de-sac.

Nick learned that Brittany and Emily, the two older Ferraro girls, now grown and on their own, had no contact with their father. Maybe the children blamed him for their mother's death, and it broke up the family.

"It's a shame about that family," a neighbor told Nick. "They were a close family, and Denise was a good mother most of the time. She had a problem, you know. I mean, did she ever get enough support to keep her illness at bay? It's tough when you have kids. They always come first," she added. "We would have them over for Christmas cookie parties, they were nice people. I understand Brittany hosts Thanksgiving for her siblings, but she and Emily want nothing to do with their father. So sad," she put her head down.

Brittany was married, working as a nurse, and living in the Harrisburg area. Emily moved in with her boyfriend in Manayunk and was working as a clerk at a funky resale clothing store favored by college students. Nick's next tactic would be to try to talk with them. In cases like this one, family members usually held onto a lot of valuable information.

"I spoke with the neighbors," Nick told Walt, and I'm getting a feeling that your instincts may be right. I also have the lab running DNA on the pill bottle. The problem with the DNA tests is that Cas lived there, so of course his fingerprints would be all over the place. You know he worked on the ambulance squad, and most of the responders to the scene were his buddies," he added.

"That's part of what bothers me," Walt said. He had a sick feeling about this case, and, as he placed a lifetime of work mementos into the boxes, he felt grateful that Nick had agreed to look into it again. After years on the force, there was an intuitive feel about these cases. A too slick husband, bawling his eyes out at the scene? That was something Walt thought deserved at least a second look.

Nick felt as though this investigation was something he could do for his Uncle, and he would leave no stone unturned in getting to the bottom of it.

Chapter 29

The Bishop Frances Reunion was moving along well, at least according to the expression on Mary Ann Redds beaming, full face. She had left no detail excruciatingly contemplated. After the truly delicious pasta (Tooty's knows how to make Italian), things were looking up for Grant and the kids.

Grant struck up a conversation with the guy at the next table, who was also a big coffee snob, and they realized that they had toured the same coffee plantation in Costa Rica, in search of the most perfect cup of coffee. Stacey could only hope that the rest of the evening would be pleasant and uneventful.

She truly looked stunning for the event. Accented in Bishop Frances gold and white, in a pearl color form-fitting Strada dress with pearls along the neckline. She wore her Phanolo Platnik skin tone heels that gave her five inches on her petite frame. She had her hair professionally styled in an chignon, and her skin was still holding onto color from the summer. Her weight was down from a few weeks ago when she was chewing and spitting with abandon, and so many people noted that she "got better with age," which she took as a big compliment.

More than that, she was happy with herself. Except for her nightmare with Cas back in her life, she had become the woman she wanted to be. If there was a little tinge of sadness that kept creeping into her heart as the night wore on, it was that her parents were not alive to share in this memorable occasion. Stacey Falesh-Gutton, the little girl who didn't even "belong" in the Bishop Frances orbit, and needed special permission to enroll, has returned victorious, if slightly flawed, like Caesar. Indeed, it was time for the great orations of the evening.

Mary Ann whispered in Grant's ear "it's time," and he rose to his feet, making his way to the podium with the children. At the same time, Cas stood up and also moved to the dais. Stacey was surprised to feel that even in this modest setting, she was getting weak in the knees.

Mary Ann spoke first: "Hello everyone, attention, attention. At this time, I would like to make a special presentation. The reunion committee—"

"What committee, Mary Ann," Larry interrupted her, "you know you did everything for this thing tonight." Once again, everyone applauded Mary Ann. This was clearly her moment.

"Well," she corrected, "we did actually have a committee for this award. Six months ago I sent a call for Alumni Award nominations, and four of us got together to review the submissions. By far, the alumna who was nominated most was Stacey Falesh-Gutton, owner of the famous Golden Day Bridal Salon in Allentown and TV star on *You've Got To Buy That Dress!* Stacey, her husband Grant, and her children Chloe and Zach are here tonight. Stacey, some people who care about you very much, want to say a few words." Stacey was both delighted and terrified.

Zach went to the microphone first, "Mom, you're awesome! Congratulations. I love you," he said. Everyone clapped.

"Mom," Chloe started, "You are always telling me to do my best and aim high, and I couldn't think of a better role model than you. I love you so much." Again, the whole room clapped.

Then Grant got to the microphone. "Stacey, I don't know how you do it. You keep the house humming, you are a wonderful wife, you have raised our children so beautifully, and your success at the salon blows me away. You are truly exceptional, and I love you so much. Congratulations."

"We also have another speaker, Cas? Didn't you want to say a few words," Mary Ann asked. Mary Ann was one of those people who couldn't see how something like that would make Stacey uncomfortable. She knew, as did everyone in the room, that she and Cas had been the "it" couple in high school. Stacey's lump in her throat doubled, and she could feel the blood drain from her face. Grant was watching in slight disbelief, but he never really knew how close to marriage they had been, how much Stacey thought about Cas over the years. He certainly had no idea that in the recent weeks Cas had re-entered her life.

"Stacey, we go way back, don't we?" Cas started, with a intimate, eye-wink of a tone. You could hear a pin drop. A few of the women shot glances to each other. "I have never forgotten about you. I've thought a lot about the determination and grit that you have shown in building your business and raising your family. Those qualities were quite evident when I knew you in high school, and then in college. I remember your all night study sessions you did so that you could graduate in three years with two majors. You always had a couple of jobs, and were hustling to create a meaningful future for yourself. And well, it might be twenty years since we graduated, but you. look. amazing."

He was eating her up with his eyes, in a spell of sorts when he realized that the room was filled with people. He cleared his throat and asked the room full of former classmates and friends, "Doesn't she, everyone?" The class clapped a bit uncomfortably, some guy at the bar whistled.

Stacey's face was at once warm with gratitude and terrified with anticipation.

Cas continued. "If I had known then what an amazing woman you would become, well, I would never have left you go," he said.

Grant was getting his "are you kidding me" face on, trying to look appropriate for Stacey, but getting very uncomfortable.

Stacey whispered to Mary Ann, "can you interrupt him, Mary Ann? He seems a bit drunk." Mary Ann didn't seem hear Stacey and just looked on, smiling dumbly. Cas clearly had a couple drinks too many, and he was rambling now. If it were the Academy Awards, the "get off the stage" music would be playing.

"And look at Chloe, everyone. Oh my God, if she is not mini Stacey, then I'm a blind man. What a knockout," he added.

Grant pulled Cas's arm that held the microphone and said, "that's enough," loud enough that the microphone picked it up.

"Hey," Cas said to Grant, "back off, little guy, you got the big prize, she's going home with you," he said. No one was sure if he meant Chloe or Stacey, but either way it was an awkward moment.

Finally, party planner extraordinaire, Mary Ann Redds, went to the microphone, cleared her throat and read from her page, rather uncomfortably, "On Behalf of the Bishop Frances Reunion Committee, for your incredible professional achievement, Golden Day Bridals has been named the number one bridal salon in the entire Northeast region, we love watching you on *You've Got To Buy That*

Dress!, and we present you with First Bishop Frances Alumni Award for Professional Achievement," she finished.

Stacey made her way to the microphone, red faced, but gracious, trying to salvage the awards portion of the night by acknowledging that she could not think of a better place to come from, and that "because of Bishop Frances, I am who I am." She had a much longer speech planned that acknowledged the role her mother played in making sure she got to go to Bishop Frances, and the support of her family, but in the nervous moments when Cas took the mic and Grant confronted him, she forgot to read from her notes. She just accepted the acrylic commemorative award engraved with her name with a smile, hoping that none of what just happened looked as overwhelmingly awkward as it felt.

Nonetheless, the genuinely supportive and warm throngs of former classmates and fellow alumni applauded. There was an undeniable sense that this award moment had turned into an embarrassing one, and Stacey just wanted to get out of there as quickly as possible. Mary Ann took a photo of the family, with Stacey smiling broadly, despite dying inside, and Grant looking absolutely miserable. He was never one for an inauthentic display of emotions. As Zach would say, "Dad knows how to keep it real." Before Stacey got back to her seat, Mary Ann tagged Golden Day on Facebook and two classmates, including Lesley, already shared the photo on their Facebook pages. When she looked at the photo more closely, she could see that Cas appeared behind Grant, almost a full head taller than him, leering over her family. Well, who said a picture is worth a thousand words? That must have been before inflation and Stacey estimated that at any auction house in the world this particular photo would be worth a cool million.

Despite Larry's insistence that they come to the after party, Stacey explained that Zach had an early game, and the family slipped out of the reunion quietly. Everyone was silent for the hour and half car ride home, the kids sleeping in the back seat and Grant looking sullen as he drove. It wasn't as if he suspected anything. He just felt oddly uncomfortable about the whole night, and he just wanted to forget that this trip down memory lane happened. Stacey kept wondering if she should bring it up to shrug it off, or just stay quiet. She choose to pretend to be half falling asleep, closing her eyes off and on and saying nothing. Maybe Grant had the right idea: never go to reunions. He never even went to his graduations. Press on with the future and don't look back.

From the top of her hand bag, she could see her phone light up. Lucky she had the phone on silent. When she looked down, she saw a text from Cas, "Where'd you go? It was just getting fun." She closed her eyes hard, wondering how in the world she could make this--and him--just go away. She shut off her phone. When they finally got home--the ride seemed hours long-- everyone just went silently to bed. Grant seemed off, and Stacey tried to remember the last time they had made love.

Is this just because of Cas, or have we been broken for a long time?

Chapter 30

It was a quiet rest of the weekend, and Stacey stayed off her phone and social media. She just needed some space and separation from everything. The big changes for Golden Day and the increased demands on her time were starting to show. Most of all the stress from having Cas show up every time she turned around and the deep sense of remorse she felt about stepping outside of her marriage made her sick to her stomach. It was great to have Martin to talk to, but he couldn't fix the problems in her marriage. That would be up to her and Grant.

It came as a welcome relief that the kids did not have much going on. The break from driving them around was just what the doctor ordered. Even though Chloe had passed her driver's test, living out in the country meant winding roads, and Stacey had read about one too many accidents on the country roads from New Tripoli leading into Allentown.

She could remember two obituaries off the top of her head of young people killed nearby. Shelby Rains, a promising football player at the high school, driving his little brother to his scout meeting. He was such a nice kid, doing nothing crazy, as far as she could see from the newspaper article, but, the roads were a slick after a slight snowfall, and both of them died on impact after swerving off the road and hitting a tree. The second was Marisa Kincaid, a shy senior Stacey remembered from a bridesmaid gown fitting. She was killed in a head on collision with a tractor.

Life is just too fragile and the country roads too windy for inexperienced drivers.

Chloe had been asking about taking the car to the mall, but Stacey rarely let her drive by herself. Maybe in summer, Stacey thought. She didn't care if she was being overly cautious. She would never be able to forgive herself if anything happened to Chloe or Zach. Surprisingly, Chloe didn't resist it too much, though she would have liked to drive to the mall sometimes. Neither kids even complained about driving around with the Golden Day Bridal Salon logo all over their SUV. They were proud of their mom. With billboards going up all over the country for *You've Got To Buy That Dress!* featuring Chloe and social media exploding, Stacey and Grant were more than happy to keep her close to home.

Not only did Cas make her uncomfortable with his inappropriate comments about Chloe's burgeoning womanhood, some of Stacey's classmates and their spouses, including Mary Ann's husband, were openly ogling at her at the dinner. She knew one day would come when men would be checking out her daughter and not her, and that day was now. But she was not a bit jealous. The truth is that Stacey, botox and all, did embrace the positive aspects of aging, like being wiser and not really caring what men thought. She truly saw it as a blessing, and this Saturday, she made a big pot of vegetable soup, stayed in her "home clothes," watched four episodes of *Die Time* in a row, and tried, as the massage therapist and Kat encouraged her, to stay present.

On Sunday, due to some miracle of motherly persuasion, all four Gutton's packed into Grant's plug-in hybrid car and headed to St. Catherine's of Sienna for mass. Stacey was pinching herself that no one even complained about it. Grant always supported going to mass and often suggested it, but Zach could be especially prickly about "sitting through the hypocrisy." The last time they all got to mass, Stacey was sure Zach was going to stand up and say something when the right-to-life advocate spoke to try to enlist parishioners into joining the March on Washington coming up to fight for unborn babies. Zach was a flaming liberal, and though Stacey admired his zest for civil rights, she was mortified that one day he would simply stand up and yell something to the speaker, or worse, the priest during mass.

As they made their way into the church, Stacey was happy to see her favorite priest, Fr. Elatta as the celebrant. Partially blind, she felt a true connection to him, as he always recognized her and called her by name when she greeted him after the services.

He was a gifted storyteller and today it seemed he was speaking right to her when he said, "The good that we do will only be seen and known by the small circle of those close to us, our families, our friends, our neighbors, or in our place of work. We can fill our day with quiet acts of faithfulness, sharing our joy and love for Jesus in simple and natural ways."

Stacey let those words wash over her and she prayed for the fulfillment from her family that would carry her, instead of needing and craving constant confirmation of her value from others. She tried to make eye contact with Grant to see if he was absorbing the message as deeply as she was, but she could see his head slumped over in a deep sleep.

When church was over, they picked up a pizza and some salads, and headed home to continue the relaxed pace of the weekend. Grant snuggled up to her on the couch and said, "When I came from the rest room at the pizza shop, I saw a gorgeous woman paying her bill at the register. My first thought was 'wow' and then I realized it was you."

Stacey blushed and kissed him with a passion she thought was gone for good. She could tell he was telling her his true feelings and it made her feel loved.

As the weekend came to a close, Stacey realized that the week ahead was another busy one. Having some down time felt great, and thankfully Martin would be filling in on *You've Got To Buy That Dress!* since Stacey would be in meetings with buyers at the salon all week. The bigger salon meant more income, but also more expenses. They needed more vendors, and she wanted to make good deals to increase revenue. They also needed to deal with the increased exposure.

Have security system installed. Talk to Kat about my chewing and spitting. Breathe.

Chapter 31

As she drove to the salon, Stacey looked up and saw the billboard featuring Chloe that was placed right at the corner of Tilghman and Fifteenth Street. It was surreal. Her megawatt smile was gleaming out from a 50 foot wide billboard with Stacey small in the background looking on. The highway boards would be four times as big, making Chloe indeed bigger than life. The headline read: Prom Drama With Mama. Chloe looked absolutely gorgeous, but modest and sweet, too. Stacey stared at her image for a long time. She could feel herself welling up just thinking how wonderful it would be if her mom could just see all of this.

Martin still had not left for New York City when Stacey got to the salon in the morning. He knew right away something was wrong.

He said, "Did you SEE CHLOE? Oh my good God, you are going to have to lock her up to keep the boys from her," he added.

Stacey didn't laugh or smile.

"What's wrong, Mom, come on, you can tell me. Wait. Not Cas again. I thought he was getting the memo," he added.

Stacey recounted the entire reunion fiasco, the drunken speech, the coveting looks Chloe got at the reunion, and most of all the totally weird vibe that was now her marriage.

"Do you think Grant suspects anything?" Martin asked.

"Not really, but he's acting really quiet, and all weekend

I sensed that something was off."

She'd remembered Grant's uncharacteristic compliment and wondered if he's trying to turn up the charm out of fear over Cas.

"I've been emotionally eating and just completely stressed out over all of this. I just want it all to go away," she said. She was starting to feel nostalgic for the days when her basement was headquarters, and she was thrilled to make a fifty dollar profit on each dress.

The problem, and they both knew it, was that Cas was not going away. Martin didn't have the heart to tell her that while she was recounting all of this, Cas left his card under the door at the front of the salon with a note that he will be back to "check on the IT services."

Now that he had the contract to install and maintain IT services for all of the new businesses in the NIZ, there was no way she could tell the police he is stalking her or making her uncomfortable. He was just doing his job. And he had already seemed to charm the local law officials. He made it his duty to go to City Hall and introduce himself, even buying donuts for everyone the first day he started working with the new businesses. He was a master charmer.

He had even worked his magic on Martin before Stacey set him straight. She felt hopeless against Cas. He simply reinserted himself in her life, and she didn't know how to get him out. Stacey was upset. It was the anniversary of her mother's death and it always hit her hard every year that she was now on her own.

Martin put his arms around her. "Listen, kiddo, you have to stay upbeat. You have everything going for you. You are Stacey Falesh-Gutton, and don't you forget it," he said. He hated leaving her and he was the one person who could turn Stacey's mood completely around. He said,

"You know what? Tomorrow, let's have lunch. You need someone to confide in, and I am your person. You hear me?"

He left to catch the bus into New York for another taping. He'd be back late tonight, but he would still be the first person in the salon tomorrow. Martin was one hundred percent heart, and Stacey felt fortunate to have him in her life.

"You *are* my person, Martin. I'll try to keep it together until you get back," she half joked, and waved him goodbye.

Chapter 32

Nick Delmar was doing his due diligence in Cas Ferraro's old neighborhood. He talked with former teachers of the Ferraro children, neighbors and the former employer of Denise. No one had a bad word to say about her. She tried to be a good mother, but she had serious mental health issues, and it seemed that she was addressing them.

One of her best friends said that she only started drinking when she suspected that Cas was stepping out on her. A few of them said that he was a little too flirty with them. The last year of her life, Denise told her closest friends that she was afraid of Cas, and that if anything ever happened to her, they need to look at Cas because she would be sure that he would be responsible. Nick had to wonder why none of this information made its way into the police reports.

"It's so sad about the kids, especially Brittany and Emily," her former friend Liz said. "They were close to their mom and they were nice kids, too. Cas seemed to be going in his own direction. I hope those kids are OK, I miss them, you know? They were friends with our kids, and nothing was ever the same again after Denise died," she added.

One of the kids' teachers even confided in Nick that she often felt uncomfortable around Cas. He was always looking down her blouse or telling her how fortunate his daughter was to have "such a good looking teacher." She thought about reporting it to HR, but she felt sorry for the kids. She knew that their mother was struggling, and she didn't want to add to a challenging family dynamic.

Despite her illness Denise worked for more than ten years part time as a catering coordinator at an area hotel. Her former manager said she was one of the best employees he ever had, until her health faltered.

"She always seemed to be upset about her family, you know, like four kids were too much, and her husband put a lot of pressure on her to be perfect, or something that she wasn't," he said. "She confided in me and some of the other coordinators. Very nice woman. Smart. Funny. It's a shame what happened there."

Nick was starting to get a picture of the Ferraro family before the death of Denise Ferraro, and next he wanted to talk to the kids. But he knew that once he did that, Cas would know that the investigation had been reopened unless they said nothing to him. He couldn't be sure of that, so he needed to move forward very carefully. Without forensic evidence he would have to build a rock-solid case, and even then it was just circumstantial.

Chapter 33

It was the premiere night of the mother-daughter episode of *You've Got To Buy That Dress!* featuring Chloe and Stacey, and there was an airing party at Golden Day Bridals. Chloe's best friends from school, and Stacey's friends, vendors, customers and relatives flocked to the swanky new salon for the party.

The caterer, who ran the Golden Day cafe, created a giant cake with the show's logo on it. Tasty hors d'oeuvres were plentiful, and the champagne was flowing. It was a wonderful reason to celebrate, and Stacey was feeling excited. Chloe was over the moon. She was getting a lot of attention at school over her billboards. *People* magazine left a voicemail about a possible story, and *Seventeen* Magazine planned a feature story on Chloe that focused on having a good relationship with your mother during the teen years.

The show's theme song blared through the salon with familiar piano tune and lyrics, "You know it when you see it and everyone agrees, *You've Got To Buy That Dress!*"

The voice-over said, "On this episode, we will go behind the scenes for a mother-daughter shopping adventure for not the perfect wedding dress, but the perfect prom dress. And it's not just any mom--you know her from our wildly popular wedding episodes--the amazing Stacey Falesh-Gutton from Golden Day Bridals comes with her lovely seventeen year old daughter Chloe. If emotions are high for wedding dress shopping, we have found that they can be just as high—okay, maybe higher—for prom dress shopping. Let's meet this dynamic mother-daughter duo!"

Everyone got quiet as Stacey and Chloe entered the shot. "I think something unique will make you stand out at prom, Chloe," Stacey said.

"I don't want to stand out. I want to fit in," Chloe said. She pointed to a few popular styles and then went try them on. When she walked out in a powder blue, off-the-shoulder form-fitting dress, the party guests gasped. She was a vision and her humility made her even more beautiful.

"I don't think it looks good," Chloe said.

The style consultant disagreed. Stacey asked her what she didn't like, and when Chloe said, "I look like a bridesmaid from a bad '90s wedding," everyone roared.

Chloe was an instant hit. Her sweet exterior belied a satiric bend. When the credits rolled and Golden Day Bridals Twitter and Facebook were shown, social media lit up with thousands of new friend requests and likes. Meg could not keep up with the demand. A completely unexpected boon, the prom market and the mother-daughter combination of Stacey and Chloe was just getting started.

People were swarming around Chloe, congratulating her on such a great job, asking her to pose for photos, and so thrilled for her newfound fame. Martin was on the lookout for any unwanted party guests, and he had been watching the door all night. But when a few cute guests caught his eye, he followed one over to the cake table, and Cas slipped into the party.

Grant and Zach had just left to try to get to the end of the high school basketball game, and the crowd was starting to thin out. Martin left with his new friend, and Stacey lost track of Nancy and Lisa. When she walked across the main showroom to turn off the projector, she caught a glimpse of Cas walking up to Chloe. It took her breath away.

He had his hand on her waist and was telling her how great she was, how beautiful she looked. Chloe, ever the mannerly, pleasing person, smiled weakly, but Stacey could see she was upset. Chloe started scanning the room for Stacey.

Stacey walked over and said casually, "Hi Cas, nice of you to come." Then she calmly asked Cas if she could speak with him for a minute. They made their way to the hallway and when he realized they were alone, Cas kissed her on the lips, and complimented her appearance.

He explained, "I just wanted to come in and make sure your technology was working. I figured it would be a busy night," he said.

Stacey could not figure out how he could even know there was an event. It was by invitation only. She wondered: was he watching the salon? Did he hack into the computers? She suspected that he was able to read her emails, and this was becoming an untenable situation.

But she could provide no proof and the fact that he was, after all responsible for the IT made it even possible that he could have access. She wondered who would believe her if she complained. As usual Cas was beautifully dressed in a camel suit and an Alexander Loroy tie. He looked great, and his signature cologne was wafting toward Stacey. But Stacey was not going to let herself get distracted.

They walked to an empty showroom, and she said, "You are making me uncomfortable, Cas. Please. Can you send someone else to check the IT from now on?"

"You don't mean that," he said playfully. He pulled her to him and kissed her hard. He slid his hand under her dress, and she pushed his hand away.

"I have to go back to the party," she said.

"OK -- you are the boss. Bye, beautiful," Cas said, and he strutted out the door, smiling.

He stood in front of the large picture window taking in the scene for a few minutes and then turned and walked away. Stacey was starting to feel violated by his presence, and she was uncomfortable with his familiarity with Chloe. She just didn't like the way he was looking at her, and his mood tonight was truly odd. He wasn't angry; instead he was acting somehow victorious, almost like a Cheshire Cat with some kind of secret yet to be revealed.

Chapter 34

After everyone left, Stacey called Martin and told him what had happened. "You took your eye off the door for a few minutes, and he slipped in. Like he had been watching us," she said.

"I'm really sorry I let you down, Stacey. I promised to watch the door all night," he said. He truly did feel badly. There was always something very protective about the way he looked out for Stacey. He always had her back.

With worry in his voice, he cautioned her: "This is getting really out of hand," Martin said. "If it's OK with you, I'm going to talk with a friend I know on the police force. I won't reveal your name. I'll just get an idea of where we stand with someone like this," he said.

Martin was convinced that Cas was stalking Stacey and Chloe, and he was concerned for their safety. If this guy was just going to keep showing up and making Stacey uncomfortable, and now Chloe, he wanted to do something. He knew that people got restraining orders when they felt threatened. Maybe they could get one against Cas. Or, if that's too drastic, maybe at the least they could ask the city to reassign Golden Day Bridals IT service so that they don't have to keep dealing with this guy whose motives seem far from pure..

When Stacey got home from the airing party she was visibly shaken.

How could so much good in her life be combined with so much bad? How did this even happen?

Her mind was racing. Grant, who is usually in bed by 9 pm was sitting in the living room. He took one look at the expression on her face and he asked "Are you alright?"

This was not a question he ever asked her. As much as he loved Stacey, he was possibly the least perceptive person in the world when it came to emotions, but he could see that she was obviously struggling.

"Someone came into the salon tonight and it frightened me," she managed. "I'm just grateful Martin was there. I'm not so sure about the safety of the downtown location," she added.

There was a long silence. Grant looked angry and hurt, and finally he asked, "Someone like Casimer Ferraro?" giving her a dejected glance. She could feel the blood draining from her face. She felt the pain that shoots up her back when she is completely overcome with stress. She sat down and began to explain.

"Yes. He's been coming in unannounced for a while, and he is starting to frighten me," she said. "He says he is checking in on the IT services, but I get a sense it is more than that," she added.

Grant looked sadder than she had ever seen him. His face was ashen and suddenly looked gaunt, as though he aged ten years and lost twenty pounds in ten seconds. There was a painful silence between them that seemed to last an hour.

"Where is his wife?" Grant asked.

"She died five years ago in some tragic accident," Stacey said. She could tell he suspected that more than just unwanted visits had happened.

"Who initiated the contact, Stacey?" he asked. She insisted it was Cas.

"We ran into each other in Philadelphia, during the

strategic planning weekend. It was completely unplanned," she said, even though she was starting to believe that Cas had engineered the whole thing.

Things had been cooling between Grant and Stacey since the Bishop Frances High School reunion. She was so busy with the new salon, Chloe's stardom, and the sheer terror of Cas's presence in her life, she hadn't allowed herself to absorb how much her deception had affected their relationship. But Grant didn't want to go further with it.

He said, "Let's go to bed." They went upstairs and made passionate love for the first time in months.

Chapter 35

As promised, the next day Martin stopped by at the Allentown Police Department to see if his friend Eric was working. Eric was a nice guy that Martin had met at the park a few years ago. They both had Brussels Griffon dogs, and they bonded over their love of the adorable pint sized breed. They had gone for drinks, kept in touch, and Martin knew that Eric had a lot of experience on the force. He thought that maybe he could shed some light on this situation.

When Martin walked into the station, first thing in the morning, he saw Eric right away, working at a desk near the front of the large office.

"Hey, what brings you here? I'm used to seeing you with your little furry friend. You aren't on the wrong side of the law, are you?" Eric joked. Martin was trying to keep it light, but he was upset about the situation, and he needed advice.

"I'm actually here for a friend," Martin said.

"Oh, sure, that's what they all say." Eric was still being silly when he noticed how solemn Martin was. "What's up, Martin? How can I help you, buddy?"

Martin told him everything. Even though he left out names, Eric knew where he worked, and he was probably piecing together who he was talking about.

"The problem with this, Martin, is that technically the guy hasn't done a thing wrong," Eric said. "I mean, if you want to give me his name, I could run a check on him and see if he has any priors. That might help," he suggested.

Martin didn't know what to do. He promised Stacey he wouldn't go into too much detail, and he certainly would not reveal her identity, but she didn't say anything about Cas's identity. The situation was getting scary. It wasn't just Stacey that Cas seemed obsessed with, it was Chloe too, and Martin always took a protective, avuncular role with Chloe and Zach. He didn't want anything bad to happen to those kids.

"The guy's name is Casimer Ferraro, and he came up here from Philadelphia to work on IT for the NIZ project," Martin told him. He added, "He's just really making things uncomfortable for my boss and her daughter. I don't know what the guy's deal is. With all the business there must be in Philadelphia for IT services, what is he even doing here?"

Eric took down the information and promised Martin he would be in touch soon.

It was good to be friendly, Martin thought, and Eric had a soft friendliness to him. He was easy to talk too, but then again, Martin made friends easily. He would be the guy striking up the conversation with the perfect stranger at the airport. It's what made him good at the salon. He was truly open-hearted, and he liked meeting people. He had an old saying he liked to share with anyone who would listen: "It's not who you know, it's who you let know you." He was just hoping that his friendship with Eric could be helpful to Stacey. Someone had to help her, he thought, especially since he slipped up the night of the big event.

Martin went back to the salon and instantly started interacting with customers. The sheer number of walk-ins on any given day had quadrupled, and Martin relished meeting new people. He breezily struck up a conversation with a young woman in the beginning stages of her dress search, and he quickly offered that he thought she'd look terrific in an all-lace trumpet dress. You could see that Martin was good at his job, and he had a way with people from every walk of life.

Chapter 36

The producers of *You've Got to Buy That Dress!* could not reach Stacey fast enough. The ratings for the mother-daughter prom show were through the roof, and they wanted Chloe featured in more episodes immediately, with studio recordings beginning this week. They loved her quick wit, and based on the comments on Facebook, the Instagram hearts, and the retweets, so did the viewers.

She was an overnight sensation, and the show wanted to capitalize on the buzz. Plus, the producers thought that prom dress buyers would remember their good experience and return in the future for their wedding gown. Chloe would be a teen fashion consultant, offering commentary on the prom dress choices of the girls on the show. There was talk of a mother-daughter podcast, and even a book on mother-daughter relationships. This train was going full speed down the tracks.

Stacey was excited for Chloe, but a little concerned about how she would finish out high school if the schedule was demanding. On the other hand, it was a fantastic opportunity, and it might lead to work after college. Chloe, like Stacey is drawn to fashion and media, and this would be a great head start in a field that's hard to break into.

She called Grant and told him about the additional shows for Chloe. Grant couldn't talk long, because he was going into a meeting, but he was supportive.

"As long as she can keep up her schoolwork, the money for the show is great for college," he said.

"I know," Stacey added, and also pointed to the experience she would be getting. They would tell Chloe about it tonight, and see her reaction.

The money from just Chloe's appearances, and the advertising campaign, would be enough to pay for her first year at NYCU. Nice cash, especially for a high schooler. Stacey worried about how she would be able to take off the days from the salon to take Chloe into New York City for the tapings. She wondered to herself if maybe Chloe was responsible enough to ride the bus in New York City herself. But there was no time to really think about that now. It was another full day at Golden Day Bridal Salon.

A local newscaster was getting married, and she was coming in for her final fitting in five minutes. She had been an especially demanding customer. She wanted every inch of her superlative figure to be shown off to its best advantage, and Stacey's seamstress already made three alterations on the waist of the gown, to show off her tiny dimensions.

Here she comes, Stacey thought as the blindingly blonde woman entered with her enabling mother in tow. Her mother was beautiful; her stylish gray hair framing her face. Stacey could see where her daughter got her looks, and thought about letting herself go gray when she could hear them bickering. Both of the personalities left a bit to be desired. Patience and kindness, she reminded herself.

"Welcome!" Stacey exclaimed in a friendly tone as they entered. Lisa and Nancy gave each other eye rolls.

Stacey still had not confided any of the Cas situation with Nancy, but she wanted to. It was such a relief to at least have told Martin. She was mortified and ashamed about the whole thing, hoping that it would just go away, but she knew better than that. With Cas showing up unannounced and unexpected, maybe it was time to bring Nancy into the fold. Nancy could be trusted, and she could also be intimidating. Where Stacey was warm and always trying to please, Nancy had a way of telling people "no" that was firmer, while still respectful. Stacey never had a complaint from a customer about Nancy, even though she often overheard some pretty "tough love" conversations. Stacey chucked to herself thinking about how much of her work was psychological. Brides come into the salon with their mother, a big psychological minefield already, and then they need to find the dress of their dreams. Some days, she felt like a miracle worker. If only she could be a miracle worker to herself, she thought ruefully.

Martin, Lisa and Nancy had back-to-back appointments and even added evening hours to take care of the demand at Golden Day Bridals. It wasn't just every mother and daughter coming in for bridal wear, it was well-known celebrities from New York and Philadelphia requesting appointments for evening wear. Stacey catered to a few actresses in the past who had come to Allentown for their Academy Award gowns, hoping to remain anonymous, but now there was demand because of the quality of the clothing, expanded designer labels and the legendary Golden Day service. Or maybe the Bailey Grift dress somehow seeped into the celebrity world.

Meg had graduated from Cedar Point College and started working for Golden Day full time, commandeering a social media presence that continued to grow internationally. The Golden Day café was now open for dinner two nights a week, and wedding catering. It was as though everything Stacey attempted with the salon was turning into reality. She just had to keep her personal life from crumbling, she thought. She and Martin would be leaving for a China buying trip in a few days and more than ever she worried about Cas Ferraro. As evening hours increased she could see him leaving the restaurant across the street, giving her a silent salute. She wondered what could possibly be his next move. Cas Ferraro did not seem like the kind of many who would simply go quietly away.

Chapter 37

Nick Delmar had spoken with dozens of people who knew Denise, Cas ,and the Ferraro children. He was getting the picture that the family was close, the children were loved, but the marriage was strained. That's not uncommon when there's mental illness, and Nick knew that firsthand. His wife's family had a lot of history of depression and bipolar disease, and as a result, divorce. He remembered someone saying that challenging family situations either bring the family closer, or it breaks the family in half. In the case of the Ferraro family, it sounds like the latter.

He drove up to the hospital where Brittany Ferraro worked as an operating room nurse to try to talk with her. He realized that talking to the kids could blow his cover, but he had a feeling that Cas was the type of guy who, even if he knew he was being investigated, would believe that nothing would come of it. Cas reminded Nick of a self-important jerk, drunk with his own sense of importance, impervious to the bad impression he could make, the off-hand comment, or worse. He seemed to know just how to dial up the charm, depending on who it was he needed to impress. That's exactly what makes him so dangerous, Nick reflected.

Brandenwood Hospital was a sprawling complex that employed thousands. Nick pulled into the crowded parking lot and finally found a space for visitors in the far corner. He parked his squad car and walked to the entrance. He was always amazed at the deferential treatment he received when he was in uniform. People either flinched in his presence or treated him as though he was a priest or a famous person.

"Hello officer," a few people intoned as he made his way to the OR department. He didn't think he would ever get used to it. He was a humble public servant, and he was just doing his job.

He wasn't even sure that Brittany would be on duty, but he thought he had to try to get more information directly from people closest to the case. The nurse at the information desk seemed to size him up approvingly. Nick was tall and muscular. He had the kindest eyes and the most child-like smile that women found rather irresistible. She sat up straighter and softened her tone, noting that Brittany was in surgery, and she should be out in an hour or two.

"You never know with appendicitis," she said. "You can wait in there," she said as she pointed to a comfortable lounge where families go to wait out the surgeries of their loved ones. Curiously she asked, "May I bring you some water while you wait?" and written all over her face was the question: "What's this strapping young police officer got with Brittany?"

Her curiosity made Nick wonder what Brittany would think when she saw him. A knowing expression on her face would say a lot. Like maybe she has been waiting for the day when some striving new police officer took up her mother's case. Trained in non-verbal communication, Nick knew how to detect lying from eye contact and nervous tics. If someone pauses when you ask them a question such as, do you know who killed your mother, that usually means yes. He knew he had to go in slowly.

Denise Ferraro's death was still classified as an accident.

He had to let Brittany know that he was asked to review some old cases before they are closed for good, and, as a matter of common practice, he had to ask the family a few questions about the circumstances of her mother's death. Nick Delmar was good with sensitive situations. His own difficult family story made him especially nuanced when speaking with families, and he was often requested to talk to children in some of the most heartbreaking situations. He was a compassionate police officer, a sensitive person and, most of all, he wanted to solve this case for Uncle Walt.

As he was mulling his approach over, he could see the nurse at reception point him out to an attractive, dark-haired woman. She was tall like Cas, with olive skin and big eyes. A real beauty. Brittany looked a bit flushed when she saw Nick in the waiting room, but she walked over with poise and softly asked, "May I help you with something?"

Nick said that he was sorry to take up her time at work, and especially sorry to bring up old wounds, but he wondered if he could speak with her briefly about her mother's death.

"I'm closing out some cases for our chief who is retiring and this is something we routinely do. Would you be able to answer a few questions?" he gently inquired.

"Okay," she said hesitantly. "I wasn't there, though, so I only know what the police report says. The only two people there were my mother and my father."

"Okay, thank you. Had your mother been having a challenging time with her illness in the weeks leading up to her death?" Nick asked.

"I'm sorry to say that I really don't know. I was away at college, and had been on a study abroad trip to Italy just prior to my mom's passing. I called home about a week before she died, and we spoke briefly. I just wanted to let her know that I made it home safely from the airport," she said.

Nick could hear how distraught she sounded and how she was not angry, but she was also not very forthcoming with details. And she was polite and very sweet. He could see her eyes welling up with tears. This had to be really hard for her.

Does anyone ever really "get over" the loss of a mother? He knew the answer was no. He appreciated her time, and was impressed with her demeanor. For such a creepy guy, Cas sure had at least one especially kind, thoughtful and nice daughter.

"Thank you, Brittany. I appreciate the information," he said softly. He felt sorry for her. She wasn't the vindictive type, he could tell, and he doubted if he could get much more information from her. He would try to track down Emily Ferraro next. Maybe she had more to say. What a tragic situation, he thought to himself. He walked out of the hospital, into his squad car, and drove back to the station to add the information into his report.

Emily Ferraro answered the phone on the first ring. When Nick explained in his usual delicate manner, that the department just wanted to close up the case by asking a few questions, she was not the reticent, grieving daughter that her sister was.

"Because you think my dad did it, don't you?" she said. "Well, he will die with that secret, and I won't be at the funeral," she added.

Nick was a little taken aback. What a change from his meeting with her sister. "We don't talk. He's for him, let's just say," she said it a clipped voice.

Nick wanted to know what made her turn on her

father. "May I come by to sit down with you a bit and take a few notes for our records?" he asked.

She agreed to meet with him, at her apartment, the following evening. When Nick got there, she was polite, like her sister, asked him if he would like a drink, and suggested they sit in the living room. The apartment was sparse, but she was young, and just starting out.

Nick started slowly, "Have you always had a difficult relationship with you father?" he asked.

"No, when I was a kid, we were fine. He brought us to school, dance and sports and stuff. Things just got bad later on and I just don't think he took very good care of my mother."

Her tough exterior was starting to crack. More petite than Brittany, Emily was perhaps a little defiant by nature. She had a turned up nose and a short punk-like hairdo, and Nick could see a little tattoo of a heart with Mom on it on the back of her neck.

"Why do you say that, Emily?" he asked.

"My mom was sick, and he was in his own world. He was an EMT, you know, but he didn't use any of those skills to help my mom. And I think he cheated on her, she knew about it and it made her sad. I just don't think he cared about her anymore," she said.

"When was the last time you spoke to your mother?" he asked.

"Just a day before she died," she said softly. "She didn't sound good. I was at college and it was exam time. When I got off the phone with my mom, I tried to call my dad to ask him if he was helping her," she was clearly getting upset by recounting it. "But he never even picked up his phone," she said. "As I said, he was just in his own world," she added.

Nick asked her for any more detail on how her mom sounded on the phone, but she didn't have much.

"She sounded drunk, and confused. She said she had a headache. She got terrible migraines," she explained.

"You've been very helpful, Emily, thank you," Nick said. "I'm very sorry that I had to make you think about this again, and I'm also really very sorry for your loss of your mother."

Before he left he had one more question, "When was the last time you talked to your dad?" he asked.

"It has been a long time. We're not in touch, but I do see my sisters and brothers. Mom would want us to stay together."

He could understand how she could be resentful. Her mother died and her father seemed out of touch. It doesn't prove he did anything, but it does suggest that he is a self-centered jerk. There was one thing Nick knew for sure. The Ferraro children were good kids, and they had seen their share of grief. He wondered if Denise's parents would be willing to talk with him. If so, they may be a good source of information.

Chapter 38

Grant was unusually talkative as soon as he awoke, as though something came to him overnight. Stacey sensed that Grant knew she had let Cas in her life again. He may not have known the extent of her transgression, at least she hoped not, but he knew something was going on.

"So this weird Cas guy just shows up at your salon, Stacey?" he asked, scratching his head like an old detective movie, before he even got out of bed.

"Yeah. He has the entire city contract for NIZ, so he services all the new places."

Grant knew this because his friend Arthur had opened a coffee roasting company right next to his office, and he complained about a "big city firm" getting the IT contract.

"I just don't get why he needs the business in Allentown," he said suspiciously. "He's got the whole city of Philadelphia." Grant felt uncomfortable with this guy feeling free to walk into Golden Day Bridal Salon any time he wanted, so he suggested something. "You can use a different IT service, Stacey, I know this because Arthur isn't going with Cas's company."

Stacey didn't know this. She thought that because she got the half price rental deal, that she had to go with the company that the city provides. Cas offered to go to the mayor's office and get the details. If he did suspect that something was happening between Stacey and Cas, he was trying to stop it. Stacey appreciated that, and that he was also not asking for details. He knew that Cas was making

Stacey uncomfortable, and he was going to figure out a way to get him out of there.

Stacey hugged Grant hard, and didn't need to say a word. Her eyes communicated the deep gratitude she felt toward him. She was impressed with his show of protectiveness toward her.

When Stacey got into the salon that day, she went right back to her office. She sat quietly by herself and she thought a lot about what has been going on. Cas did her no favors, she thought. And Grant is so quietly tough. She recalled a story that Grant's parents told her about him from when he was a teenager. A dozen boys were challenged to go camping in the middle of winter as part of a confidence-building project in eighth grade. It got colder and colder as the night went on, and each hour a few more boys called their parents to go home. By the time dawn came there were only two people left in the tent: the school counselor who coordinated the program and Grant Gutton. He might have been bullied, and called "the runt" by the bigger kids before that camping trip, but after that he wasn't afterwards. Maybe Grant Gutton was all the man Stacey ever needed, she thought. The thought comforted her.

The morning was as busy as usual, and Chloe was getting a lot of media requests. Stacey was getting concerned that all of the time she was spending going into New York for the show was taking her away from her school work, but her second quarter report card came in and it was good. Stacey was hoping that all of this TV experience would help her when she applies to the most exclusive media school in Manhattan, the Gisch School and New York City University.

Martin came in with a fresh and warm cherry cobbler he had just whipped up, followed by Eric, who took a break from the police department with an update on Cas.

"The guy is clean. I couldn't even find a speeding ticket," Eric said. "The only cloud over him is that there were some raised eyebrows after his wife's accident. She had some health issues, and the one person who stood to gain from her death was Cas. But there was no autopsy, and she was cremated within a day."

Eric explained that when he reached out to the Philadelphia Police Department there was one officer looking into the case again.

"Something doesn't seem right, but there is no evidence," Eric added. "So, other than a possible homicide," he joked, "the guy's a choir boy."

Stacey stood frozen, her mouth opened in disbelief. It sounded like the preview of her favorite show, *Die Time.*

Chapter 39

Cas looked sullen and withdrawn as he entered St. Bartholomew's parish rectory. Confessions were over for the weekend, but his longtime friend, Father Mark Franchesky suggested he come anyway. When he saw Cas, looking gaunt with piercing, restless eyes, Father Mark told himself not to let his concern register on his face.

Embracing his lifelong friend, Father Mark said, "So great to see you, Cas, thank you for making the trip!" as enthusiastically as he could muster. "How are you?"

Cas, barely looking at him, his eyes filled with tears, guilt and regret, stammered, "I'm a broken man, Mark."

Mark knew that while Cas appeared to the outside world to have it all: a beautiful apartment in center city Philadelphia, a successful business, a fancy, late model sports car, and a way with the ladies, the years following Denise's death had been hard for him. For years, as Denise struggled with mental illness, he sought counsel from Father Mark, his high school friend. He had to step in and parent his children alone not only after Denise died, but also before, as her condition worsened.

And yet his two older daughters seemed to forget all of that. He'd see his friends, married and enjoying the usual highs and lows of raising families, but no one could understand the stress he was under. Denise's work history was marked with sick days and eventually disability because of her illness. None of the neighbors that Nick Delmar interviewed recounted the horrifying night Denise ran from the house stark naked, knocking on doors. But when she was good, she was good, and that's all anyone on the outside saw.

As his old high school friend, and the most compassionate person he knew, Mark became someone Cas could always turn to over the years. Mark was a patient, non-judgemental listener. Unlike other clergy, he didn't think that prayer was the answer for everything. Sometimes they just went for beers. He would urge Cas to hire live-in care for the children when Denise was not up to the task, and Cas did so off and on, but teenagers being cared for by strangers is never easy. Emily was getting into drugs, and Clark had serious learning disabilities.

In the aftermath of Denise's death, Mark watched helplessly as Cas' life fell apart. His children pulled away from him, neighbors whispered about his possible role in her death, and all the women he once playfully approached for affection went running for the hills. He was even the subject of a thinly veiled #metoo post that went viral. A former employee alleged that "a wife killer hit on me," and everyone in the area knew who she was talking about. His business was faltering in Philadelphia, and he was forced to look for IT contracts far beyond Philadelphia just to keep up the tuition payments for Renee at boarding school, and to maintain his affluent lifestyle. His parents provided no "blood is thicker than water" unwavering support.

"I have nothing," Cas, in a half whisper, head bowed, said to his old friend. "I am lonely, and I'm a stranger in my own family. More and more I'm an outcast to society," he added. Casimir Ferraro, who insisted on perfection from himself, his wife, and his estranged children, had become at best the perfect middle aged cliche, and at worst a lying, cheating murderer.

Mark, the soft-hearted priest, who had heard just about everything in the confessional over the years was not sure what he could do for his friend, but he was filled with worry, and the Holy Spirit, and he hoped to alleviate some of the pain Cas felt.

"Let's begin with a prayer," he suggested. Softly, Fr. Franchesky began, asking Cas to repeat after him: "Oh most heavenly God, Prostrate at your feet, I implore your forgiveness," Father Franchesky said. Cas repeated it in a barely audible voice.

In unison the men prayed aloud together, sitting face to face: "I sincerely desire to leave all my evil ways and to confess my sins with all sincerity to you and to your priest. I am a sinner, have mercy on me, Oh Lord. Give me a lively faith and a firm hope in the Passion of my Redeemer. Give me, for your mercy's sake a sorrow for having offended so good a God. Mary, my mother, refuge of sinners, pray for me that I may make a good confession. Amen."

Tears were streaming down Cas's face and he began to sob.

"Bless me Father for I have sinned. It has been many years since my last confession. I have been a wicked man," Cas said, dropping from his chair, to his knees. He finished his confession, and Father put his hand on his friend's hand, and encouraged him to repent his sins. When the confession was over, his lifelong friend and priest, visibly shaken, told Cas to beg the Lord for forgiveness, say the novena, and pray the Rosary each day. He helped Cas to his feet, and invited him to the rectory kitchen for dinner. They ate in silence, and Cas left, still with his head bowed, into the dark night alone.

Chapter 40

Stacey was packed for her big trip to China and India with Martin, and drove Chloe to the early bus for New York City for Chloe to make the trip all by herself. They had gone into the city dozens of times together, and she knew what to do as soon as the bus got to Port Authority. *You've Got To Buy That Dress!* always provided a sleek, black car waiting for her as she exited 43rd Street. They hugged for a long time.

Stacey hated to leave for China and then India, but if the salon truly wanted a global inventory of the latest bridal fashions, then it had to be done. It would be a relatively quick trip to China--one week--considering the distance, and Stacey had the itinerary planned down to minutes to maximize the time. When the buyer suggested that they go right onto to India, Stacey at first refused.

"That's ridiculous. Too much to do in one trip," Stacey had said. But the Indian bridal companies picked up the cost of the entire trip from China to India for her and Martin, and Stacey couldn't say no. That alone would be the cost of several dresses, and it would take the salon a long time to make up the cost of travel.

Two weeks away from Chloe, Zach and Grant would be the longest Stacey ever left her family, but she knew it made sense to just do it.

"Be safe, Mom," Chloe said. Zach looked up from his phone and took his earplugs out.

"Be safe in New York., Chloe," he said. Zach was such

a sweet kid. He truly loved his sister, and it touched Stacey to see him worried about her.

Blood is thicker than water.

When Stacey pulled up to school with Zach, two of his buddies were waiting for him. He was popular, and he had a nice group of friends who seemed to look out for each other. Stacey was glad that he was having a good year and that he had friends he could rely on. Like Chloe, Zach knew that this was a monumental goodbye--he wouldn't see his mom for two weeks--and he hugged her tight.

"Be careful, Mom. Bring me back something Chinese," he said. They both laughed, knowing the reference from their favorite Christmas movie, *Home Alone*.

"Take care of Dad and Chloe, okay," she said. She could feel her eyes welling up. She loved her family so much. They were everything to her, and leaving them for this long made her stomach ache.

When she got to the salon, Grant was waiting to drive her and Martin to the airport so that they wouldn't have to pay for airport parking. Martin seemed excited for the trip, but a little nervous too. It is a long trip from Philadelphia to Beijing and then off to India, and he hoped to be able to sleep for part of it at least. For that reason he kept himself awake most of the night, and for once he looked his age. When they got to the airport, Grant told Stacey that everything would be OK at home. Grant knew she was nervous, and he wanted to assure her that everyone would be fine in her absence.

"I love you, Grant," she said. He looked at Martin and said, "Both of you, be safe."

He watched as Martin and Stacey disappeared into the crowd, and he drove off. His parents had already left for Florida, so he was on his own with the kids, but he didn't think it would be so hard. They were getting older, and Chloe should already be in New York by now. Like clockwork, his phone went off, as instructed.

"Safe at Port Authority," Chloe typed.

Grant typed back: "OK, good. Text me when you get to the studio. Love, Dad."

Chloe made fun of how Grant signed off on his texts, as they were a letter. The next stop for Grant Gutton that day would be the mayor's office. He had to get Cas Ferraro out of his wife's life.

The black car was waiting for Chloe outside of Port Authority, just as the producer said it would be. A sign for the show was on the front window and when Chloe got into the car, the driver started toward the production studio. Chloe could see a tray of snacks, Perrier, and soft drinks. She thought this is definitely something she could get used to. This was her first big trip into the city, and she felt so grown up. If she could graduate from high school right now and begin her career in media in NYC, she would. But she also really wanted to go to NYCU, so this, she thought, was just incredible experience to take with her. She enjoyed the celebrity treatment, and usually spent the ride texting her friends back home, instagramming photos of the city, and tweeting how ridiculously lucky she was to be in the city instead of struggling her way through another remedial algebra class.

As promised, Chloe texted Grant "made it to the studio," and Grant felt a wave of relief wash over him. He knew Stacey was still at the airport, so he let her know that Chloe made it to the studio. Stacey was still making her way through security when the text came through. "Thank God," she texted back to Grant and "love you."

As soon as Chloe got to the studio, the hair and makeup

crew were waiting for her. The producers planned for her to wear a bright red prom gown by Boey Stray. The dress had a strapless bodice with rhinestones randomly sprinkled throughout.

She looked so grown up and was a natural in front of the camera. The producers suggested a few clip-in blonde highlights in her chestnut hair, and without asking her mom for permission, she told them to do it. Her hair was styled in the new "beachy wave" look, and even though most TV people rely on heavy make-up, Chloe didn't need much.

The shoot took longer than expected, and the producers asked if she could come back in the morning. She had school the next day, which she was happy to miss, but what would her parents say? Chloe called Stacey, and she said that as long as she could make up the work from school over the weekend, she could stay over. The producers assured Stacey that it would be safe. The producers took care of the transportation to the luxurious Four Seasons hotel, room service for dinner, her overnight stay, and her transportation back to the studio the next morning. They even had an overnight bag with fashionable clothes in her size ready for her by the time the shoot was over. Chloe was feeling like a star, and *You've Got To Buy That Dress!* was soaring in the ratings.

When the shoot was over the next morning, Stacey got a long email from the producers. The show was spinning off a new line of casual clothes, and they wanted Chloe to be the model and spokesperson.

Stacey immediately reached out to Chloe's teacher to discuss how her daughter would finish high school with the new opportunities that were before her. Stacey wanted Chloe to enjoy this incredible moment, but to also keep two feet on the ground and achieve academic success.

She was concerned about the extra time off, but Chloe's teachers seemed to reassure her that she could make up the material and that she was excelling in school. The time away would not hurt her academically, and Stacey knew that the opportunity to work in television on a hit show would really help Chloe make her way in the media world. Still, Stacey's own life was proof that academics had to come first, and she did not want Chloe's future compromised because of missed schoolwork.

The trip was going fast. Stacey prided herself on light packing and decided that if she bought anything too big for her suitcase, she would just ship it back to the states. The flight went smoothly and surprisingly quickly. Both Martin and Stacey nodded off within an hour of take-off. Martin woke up for dinner, but Stacey slept until she heard the captain say that they would be landing in Beijing in less than an hour.

Chapter 41

Grant had a good meeting with the mayor's assistant. The mayor, however, swamped with a new investigation of his office, would not be able to meet with Grant for a month to discuss Cas Ferraro's handling of Golden Day's IT services. Grant asked if anyone else could help and the mayor's assistant said that in a week or so, she would be in touch with the name of the person who was on leave and would be returning. Disappointed that his request could not be handled immediately, Grant left. He had two weeks till Stacey returned, hopefully it will be done by then, he thought.

Grant worried that with Chloe receiving attention from every possible media outlet for *You've Got To Buy That Dress!* Zach might be feeling left out. And with Stacey away for her international buying expedition for two full weeks, Zach would be missing her more than he would ever admit.

Grant knew what it was like to be second best. His parents had always heaped praise on his younger brother Garth to no end. Growing up, Garth was the improved version of Grant's "sloppy copy" as they say in writing class. It was as though they had given parenting a dry run on Grant, and with Garth they got all the details right. Taller, more athletic, with bright blue eyes and a megawatt smile, girls swarmed around him from middle school on. Betta always cackled at his jokes, and praised his good looks, "He looks just like my father," she would say.

Yes, Grant had sympathy when it came to being

overlooked, so he texted Zach, asking if he could pick him up after school so they could have dinner together and maybe play a few games at the local bowling alley. Zach was thrilled with the idea. Grant rarely left the office before 5:30, but at 2:30 he shut off his computer, grabbed his Land's End puff coat, and headed into the cold to have some father-son time with his only son.

"Looks like there's no one even here," Zach said as they pulled into the Allen Bowling Lanes.

Grant had so many fond memories of working in a bowling alley as a teenager. His Uncle Anthony had taken him under his wing, and gave him a job. Uncle Anthony was a gentle, fatherly mentor to Grant. He taught Grant about bowling alley maintenance and how to handle unhappy customer. In many ways Grant was like his Uncle Anthony. He was hardworking and not very expressive about his emotions. He had a natural propensity for kindness, and people were drawn to him. Where Stacey was always in "what's next" mode, Grant was somehow gentler and softer, always giving people the benefit of the doubt. Grant was not overly reflective about the passage of time, but he thought that Zach seemed lonely lately with Stacey spending more time at the salon, and his sister's newfound fame.

They played three games, and Grant had won two. "We need a tiebreaker," Grant said.

"Can I get some French fries? I'm starting to get hungry," Zach asked. What was nice about Allen Bowling was that the staff brought your food right to your lane. You just order it from a computerized screen. Zach and Grant ordered a pizza and French fries, and Grant even got a beer. It was shaping up to be a big night for the Guttons at Allen Bowling, and Grant was in a rare, relaxed mood.

"That was fun, Dad," Zach said on the way home. "I love you," he added.

"You got much homework, Zach?"

"Only English," he said, and they rode the rest of the way in a warm, comfortable silence.

Chapter 42

China was everything Stacey had imagined.

As soon as they got off the plane, Martin spotted his friend, Wang Wei, whom he met years earlier when Allentown hosted Chinese journalists for a week. Of course, Martin kept in touch and Wang Wei, delighted with the prospect of seeing his friend from the United States, graciously offered to take Martin and Stacey around the city and even host them at his high-rise in the center of Beijing. That's Martin.

In addition to the business they had come to Beijing to do, Wang Wei insisted on showing them the sights, so Martin and Stacey allotted the first day for an informal trip to The Forbidden City, the Summer Palace, and the Temple of Heaven. Wang Wei wanted them to bike through Beijing, but Stacey put her foot down and said that she was too frightened to be on a bike with nine million other people in a packed city. Everywhere she turned throngs of people confronted her, hundreds of people, many wearing masks to avoid inhaling the contaminated air. Sheets of people crossing the cavernous street at a time. If she looked or stepped away for a second, and she and Martin could be separated. Her phone still wasn't working, and many taxi drivers did not speak English.

Martin was surprised to see Stacey so unsure of herself, but as much as Stacey wanted to see the world, she was fundamentally a home body, and since Cas had re-entered her life, she had a caution to her that made her rethink her every move. Wang Wei warned both of them that the Chinese people may ask to take their photos. Chinese people were calling Stacey by the name of the actress Reese Witherspoon, though she could not see any resemblance.

"It's the blond hair and blue eyes," Martin said. You are like an exotic animal here. And Martin, too.

Finally, after a full day of touring and acclimating to the time difference, it was time to meet with the Bespoke Tailors who promised Stacey incredible deals on custom-made wedding gowns for the most discerning bride. If a woman came into the salon asking for something that Stacey could not provide, she could suggest something custom, from China. According to Martin, with the right negotiation, it could even cost less than an off-the-rack gown.

Stacey couldn't believe the value. The way it worked is that a bride could describe what she wants, send in her measurements, and the Chinese tailors would create something to her exact specifications. There was no bridal salon in the US offering this service, and Stacey knew that it would continue to put Golden Day on the map. They offered her a chance to try it out by imagining a dress, giving her measurements, and within a couple of hours, the one-of-a-kind silk creation was made. She slipped into the off the shoulder silhouette and Martin said, "I think this international travel has had a positive effect of your waistline."

Stacey did look svelte and, somehow taller. She wanted the gown, and, as a courtesy, Bespoke simply gave it to her: a dress that might cost two thousand in US, was hers free.

"Don't you wish you brought another suitcase?" Martin asked. But Stacey shipped the dress home, again, on the dime of Bespoke. After a few hours going over the procedures for the custom dresses, Stacey and Bespoke struck a deal and signed the paperwork to be the exclusive US distributor for Bespoke custom gowns.

They left, and Wang Wei insisted they go for Hot Pot. Stacey hardly ate a bite. She was starving when they got back to the apartment. Sensing that she wasn't eating enough, Martin pulled out an all-natural granola bar from his coat pocket and gave it to her.

"I have more where this came from, little one," he said. Stacey felt grateful, but also knew that one sugary granola bar would lead to two, three, four and she would be walking the streets of Beijing looking for sweets once she started. So she said, "thanks, Martin, but I'm fine," and put a piece of sugar free gum in her mouth instead.

Before they left China they both headed to the Pearl Market where Martin got not one, but three custom made suits and made-while-you-wait prescription glasses. He looked great, but Stacey could not help but to laugh out loud when she saw him coming toward her with a new piece of rolling luggage, also from the Pearl Market, to carry it all back. He was so much fun to travel with, but this was just the first leg of their international adventure. As they left the Pearl Market, Stacey spotted a mother and daughter selling beautiful silk scarves, and she was awash in longing for her family. Missing Grant and the kids was starting to make her irrationally buy things for Chloe and Zach, like a hand-carved chess set and a pearl ring that Stacey doubted Chloe would even wear.

I miss my family.

Chapter 43

Stacey was feeling homesick, but she didn't want to say anything to Martin. He was doing his best to keep her entertained, buy everything in sight, and distract her from Cas and her family fending for themselves at home. Before they left for the airport, she FaceTimed with Grant and the kids. She could feel herself tearing up when Grant's face filled the screen on her computer.

"I miss you, Grant," she said. He looked at her with a warmth that touched her heart in a way she hadn't felt in a long time. His dark eyes crinkled up at the sides and he seemed so thrilled to lay eyes on her.

"There's my little doll--all the way in China--how are you?' he said.

"Hi, Mom," Zach said casually. "Granny and Pop-Pop are selling the Florida condo," he added. It was true that Isaac seemed to have enough of retirement life in Florida. They'd be moving back to the area, looking for a place near Stacey and Grant. Pop-Pop just wants an apartment, but Granny wants a house. Stacey wasn't really surprised, but nor did she care. She just wanted to see Grant, realizing that being away from him shocked her into the actuality of how much she loves and misses him.

"Maybe I should come to India and bring you home," Grant only half teased.

"I wish you could, Grant, I had enough of this. I don't want to travel so far without you again," she said.

After they hung up, Grant realized that no one from the

mayor's office had gotten back to him about re-assigning Golden Day's IT service. He needed to follow up.

As soon as they landed in India, Stacey felt relief not only to have Martin with her, but to be on the second and final part of her world travels. As much as she was fascinated by the different cultures, she just wanted to go home. India was as thrilling as it was exhausting, a constant roller coaster of sensory overload.

After their meeting with the bridal designers in Delhi, a few men even asked Stacey to pose for a photo with her. She didn't like the way she was being surveyed from head to toe. She dressed more modestly than ever, but still she felt as though their eyes were looking right through her, and it made her nervous.

The streets were more crowded than anything she had ever seen. Fifth Avenue had nothing on New Delhi any day of the week. Throngs of people, thousands of merchants of every kind, lined the streets, and the markets in India is a full-on cultural immersion. Stacey's eyes almost glossed over when she walked into a store that held what must have been fifty thousand delicately detailed tunics.

The intricate and regal bridal styles, with their hand sewn embellishments, were like nothing her brides back home have ever seen. Stacey was sure she had gotten deep discounts that she could turn over to her customers and use to reap higher profits. The move had been expensive, and except for the disruption and despair of having Cas back in her life, it had been worth it.

The new salon was opulent, but stark compared to the seven-star hotel she and Martin were staying in that was quite simply the most luxurious structure she had ever seen except for the Taj Mahal. Carpet so thick she thought of lying on the floor for nap had it not been for the exquisite feather bed and hand embroidered bedspread.

In addition to the gorgeous bridal couture that would be shipped by the end of the month, and the goodies she picked up in China, she was bringing home thoughtful mementos for her Grant and the kids. A stunning, sequined tunic for Chloe, a book on Indian politics for Zach, and a handmade stoneware coffee mug for Grant.

She pondered the sharp contrasts of India. Within a block of their fabulous hotel, there were impoverished children, playing in mud, begging for rupees. As she considered the contrasts, she realized that it is not unlike Allentown, or any other American city. The grandness of the hockey arena, her own salon, and the upscale restaurants were all within a few blocks of broken down row homes, and abandoned, boarded-up housing.

She and Martin were treated like royalty, and their week in India, was coming to a close. Most of the people she met were incredibly gracious, and the food was the most delicious she had ever eaten. She much preferred the vegetarian friendly Indian food to the Chinese food. She had absolutely no desire to chew and spit in India.

Whenever she traveled like this, she wished her family were with her. She made a note to herself that in the future, she would find a way to bring everyone. She was happy to be leaving for home in the morning, and her clothes were hanging on her. She loved the Indian cuisine, and the many vegetarian offerings, but even though the food was plentiful, she ate only enough to not be hungry at each meal, and it showed. When she returned the scale read 134.

Well, one thing in my life is going well.

Stacey promised herself that she would use the positive momentum from the trip and get help for her eating disorder. On the plane home, she splurged for in-flight internet access and read as much as she could about her rare, but growing issue.

She learned that Chewing and Spitting, often referred to as CHSP, is a form of disordered eating where someone chews food, but spits it out rather than consuming it. The food that is often chosen is food that is considered junk: cakes, cookies, chocolate and other sweets. Chewing the food and then spitting it out can give the person with the eating disorder a sense that no food is off limits and some eating disorder websites have comments from people with this eating disorder that state that chewing and spitting help to maintain a lower weight because they can enjoy the foods they can't eat without gaining weight. But this, ultimately is false. According to medical experts, the sight, smell, thought and taste of food triggers the cephalic phase of gastric secretion which prepares the body for digesting good and even though the food is not swallowed, CHSP increases stomach acids, can erode teeth and can alter metabolism.

Stacey vowed to not allow her sense of having an overwhelming life—full-tilt career, a demanding family life, and perhaps most of all, the deep sense of loss she still felt over the deaths of her parents— to affect her eating and her health. She promised herself that she will get the help she needs to overcome her eating issue. That's one of the great benefits of travel, she realized. A change of scenery and a chance to view her life objectively and away from the day to day stresses gave her renewed hope for a fresh and healthy start.

Now if I could just do it.

Grant picked up Stacey and Martin from the airport and Stacey was overjoyed to see the whole family in her Golden Day Bridal SUV. Chloe burst out crying when she saw her mom after two long weeks, and Zach embraced her with a ferocity she never felt. Grant rushed everyone into the vehicle, afraid he might be charged for double parking, but Stacey could see the warmth in his eyes, double parking charge or not.

My family.

Chapter 44

Nick Delmar drove to a stately Federal style home in Olyphant, a lovely suburb of Scranton, where Denise Wasnitsky grew up. The professionally landscaped yard, the regal columns and the well-manicured lawns of the surrounding homes, signaled that this was where those who had made something of themselves in the hardscrabble Northeastern area of Pennsylvania lived.

Gene Wasnitsky had long since retired as a phone company executive, and his wife Ann took only the occasion interior design assignment on referral from family or friends to keep her mind on something positive. They were accommodating over the phone, and Nick sensed that talking about their daughter's death would be difficult, and yet in some ways therapeutic. No one ever knows how to bring up the subject of a deceased child, but most parents who have lived through the worst grief known say it is good to talk about it.

Gene's health was failing, and Ann asked if he could come early afternoon so that it would not be too late. Nick knocked on the door, and within a few seconds, Ann Wasnitsky came to the door. She was a petite brunette, stylishly dressed in the upscale flowy activewear that have become popular. In her early seventies, she exuded a proper, polished demeanor. Their well appointed home was spotless and comfortable with a large fireplace in the main sitting room, where Nick was invited. Ann had prepared tea and set out a tray of cookies and candies.

"Thank you for seeing me," Nick said. "I'm so sorry about your daughter," he added.

"It's so hard for us to believe she's gone, even these years later," Ann said. A large pastel color portrait of Denise, their only child, dominated the wall above the mantle. Gene Wasnitsky fought back tears as he described a young girl, full of life, who wanted to become a nurse.

"She passed all of her tests, but she just could not get beyond the emotional attachment she felt with so many of the patients," he said. "She'd come home too upset to even eat dinner after a day of working with patients facing fatal diagnosis. She had a heart of gold. Her Brittany followed in her footsteps," Gene added proudly.

"I have spoken with both Brittany and Emily," Nick said. "That's why I wanted to come to talk with you. If it isn't too much for you, can you tell me a little bit about Denise's mindset and her health at the time of the accident?" he asked gently.

Ann began, "She was a little overwhelmed with the kids, I mean who wouldn't be with four, but it seemed to be getting a bit easier when the two older girls were away at college. I thought she had been doing better," she added. She talked about Denise feeling depressed, getting some medication, and doing a lot better, but in the days before she passed away, she seemed to slip into a deeper depression.

"I called her the day before the accident," Gene said, and Ann corrected him.

"You mean before she died." They shot each other fitful glances, with Gene shaking his head and trying to offer an explanation.

He offered, "Ann's never really accepted that Denise fell."

"Could you tell me more about that," Nick tried to be gentle, he could see that these were two very decent people who were still grieving.

Gene offered, "We loved Cas when we first met him. He was an ambitious guy from a good family, and we could see that Denise was head over heels for him. She had a lot of boyfriends, but she fell hard for Cas. He was devoted to her in the first few years of their marriage, but after the kids came, he seemed interested in other things."

"Other things meaning other women," Ann said angrily. "He made a fool of our daughter. Everyone knew but her that he was running around. He even had a fling with one of their babysitters," she said as she started to sob.

Gene went into the kitchen and brought out a box of letters that Denise had written to her parents as the marriage was starting to unravel. He handed his wife his handkerchief from his pocket and she began to absorb her tears into it. Gene, despite his failing health, was the perfect gentleman, and Nick could see that he adored Ann. This was a good family that had to endure the unspeakable: the loss of a daughter.

Anyone who ever has to go through something like this, deserves a pass on most things.

"Here's a letter where she writes that she is afraid of Cas," Ann said: "Dear Mom and Dad, Cas has been verbally abusive, and I don't know what I'm going to do." The letter was dated a year before she fell to her death.

"Find the one about the antifreeze," Gene said.

Ann rifled through the plastic box and found the one that read: "I don't know what to make of my feelings. Maybe I'm just paranoid. Yesterday when I went into the kitchen for coffee, I saw Cas pouring antifreeze into a water bottle. He seemed startled to see me. I was too frightened to ask him about it. I have been feeling so sick lately and I haven't been drinking. I've been taking all of my depression medication, and emotionally I have been feeling a little better." That letter was dated two weeks before she died.

"I know she had blood work done at the hospital less than a week before she died," Ann said. They were both still distraught about their daughter's death, and they didn't know what to make of the circumstances.

Could Cas have played a role? The Wasnitsky's didn't want to think the worst of their son-in-law, but his behavior during the marriage and since their daughter's death had them disillusioned and concerned. They told Nick about the affairs during the marriage that Denise found out about through neighbors, even their own children.

"He carried on with Brittany's seventh grade teacher for years and everyone at the school knew about it but Denise," Ann said.

"And after she died, he sold the house, gave away all her things, and bought himself a red Camaro," Gene's voice was starting to break.

"And we never hear from him," Gene added.

"Not even a Christmas card. The grandchildren keep in touch, especially Brittany and Emily," Ann said. Clearly the unthinkable events of their daughter's life have contributed to their own ill health and despondency. Nick thought he should be direct.

"Do you suspect foul play?" he asked.

"Yes, we do," they both said in unison.

"But it seems impossible to prove," Ann added. "We've hoped for a deeper investigation for years, but how do you convince the police to do it?"

Nick assured them that he would find the truth about

what happened to their daughter. "I'm not going to give up until I find out what truly happened on the day Denise died," Nick said.

The gratitude in their eyes was all the pay or thanks Nick Delmar needed. He left, promising to keep the Wasnitskys updated on the investigation into the death of their beloved daughter, Denise Wasnitsky Ferraro. Gene and Ann held each other and watched Nick's car pull away.

Chapter 45

Cas pulled up to the Port Authority Bus Terminal chauffeured car line with an exact replica of the sign for *You've Got To Buy That Dress!* displayed on the dashboard, his chauffeur hat obscuring most of his face. He double checked the show schedule he pulled from Stacey's computer and knew that at any moment, Chloe would emerge from the terminal doors, a clone of her mother at that age.

Stacey is a bit long in the tooth anyway. If the president can have a pretty young thing on his arm, so can I. All truly successful men attract much younger ladies. Deep down, Chloe is probably just like her mommy: a little bit naughty.

He waited, aroused by the thought of the fresh-faced, sweet Chloe entering his car. Like clockwork, just when he expected, Chloe came out into the crisp New York air, her bright eyes enthusiastic and innocent. She noticed the car waiting for her and piled into the back with her overnight bag, excited for two days of stardom!

There were always different drivers, so it made no difference to Chloe who was at the wheel. He simply nodded to her, said a quick "good afternoon, miss," and drove away.

Chloe was beaming and keyed up for the days ahead. She could feel the drudgery of high school ending and the excitement of going to college and working in New York City ahead of her. Her dreams were coming true, and she knew that a career in TV or fashion—hopefully both—

would be the direction she was moving in. *I'm so lucky!* Her cell phone buzzed with a new text.

It was from her mom. "Are you in New York yet?"

"Yep! On way to studio now!"

Chloe took a photo of a woman walking five dogs and posted it on her Instagram. She took a selfie and tweeted, "can't wait to see the new prom gowns!"

The producers of *You've Got To Buy That Dress!* loved her use of social media, and she had hundreds of new followers every time a new episode aired. She was texting her friends and scrolling through posts. Forty-five minutes passed before Chloe wondered what was taking so long. Usually, the drive took twenty minutes to the studio.

"Are we almost there?" She asked cheerfully. She had been so engrossed in social media that she didn't realize how much time had passed.

"Yes, here we are," Cas said as he pulled up to a large warehouse Chloe did not recognize. "The studio has moved. I'll show you in," he added.

Chloe had no reason not to believe him, so she got out of the car with her bags and began to follow Cas. As he walked ahead of her, obscuring his face with his scarf, she began to get frightened. It was a desolate area, with no other cars or signs of life.

"Where's Mary Ellen?" she asked. He made no reply as he kept walking, leading her to the rusted door of a run down building. "Where are we going?" she asked again, her voice cracking.

Cas grabbed her by the hand and pulled her into the door. Inside it was pitch black, and Chloe began to panic.

Cas said, "Scream all you want, but no one will hear you." Chloe reached for her phone but Cas already had his hand in her bag. He took her phone out and smashed it with a hammer. Chloe began to cry.

He ordered Chloe to sit and taped her wrists, as he pulled her arms behind her and strapped her to the chair. In the pitch darkness, Chloe could see nothing but some dirt on the floor. The room appeared to be empty.

"Your mother wants me out of her life, so I need to get her attention. Besides, you look just like her," Cas said. Chloe's mind was racing, and she was sure she had heard his voice before, but where? She closed her eyes and tried to think. The man walked away, locking the large door behind him. Chloe began to pray, sobbing and searching her mind for where she had heard that man's voice.

Chapter 46

Mary Ellen, the producer of *You've Got To Buy That Dress!* was upset that Chloe was almost an hour late. Every hour of studio time cost the producers thousands of dollars in rental fees. She was beginning to think that maybe they should have gone with a professional actress for this prom series. She called the chauffeur company, and Raymond, the manager, took her call immediately.

"I'll call the driver right now," he said. "Would you like to wait on the line?"

Mary Ellen waited only a few minutes when Raymond came back to the line to tell her that the driver was still on the que for Chloe at Port Authority. "Sometimes buses are late, ma'am," he said.

But Mary Ellen knew something must be wrong. Chloe was never late, even if she was an amateur. She really enjoyed being on the show, and she took it seriously. She called Stacey to confirm that Chloe had made the 8 a.m bus into the city, as planned.

Stacey immediately panicked. Something in the pit of her stomach told her that she should. She knew this was an ominous situation because she had the text from Chloe, telling her that she was in the chauffeured car, on the way to the studio more than an hour ago.

"What do you mean she never showed up?" she wailed. She scrolled through her texts and read out loud what Chloe had typed: "Yep, on my way to the studio now!"

Stacey frantically dialed Grant and he abruptly left his

weekly team meeting, running down Hamilton Street to the salon within minutes. He phoned 911 in the meantime and shouted, "Our daughter Chloe is missing!"

The emergency operators alerted not only the Allentown Police Department and the Philadelphia Police Department, but also the New York City Police Department. Nick Delmar called Stacey and was taking down her statement over the phone, as he made the trip north to Allentown, squad car lights blaring, ignoring every traffic law on the books. Martin, always a man of action, had called Eric from the Allentown Police Department and told him what was happening.

"It's Cas Ferraro, I know it," he told Eric. Eric thought that Cas was a credible lead. The video from the Bishop Frances High School Reunion, where Cas Ferraro creepily praised Chloe's appearance, had gone viral on YouTube. The comments ranged from, "Yep, she's a hottie" to "What a old creep, keep her away from HIM!" In no time, news channels from New York, Philadelphia, Allentown, and even CNN and Fox had Chloe's photo on the screen.

"Young star of *You've Got To Buy That Dress!* never reported for today's show taping, leading authorities to believe that she has been kidnapped. A person of interest is Cas Ferraro, a family acquaintance, who had admired the teen's appearance and was seen lurking around her mother's now internationally famous Golden Day Bridal Salon in Allentown, Pennsylvania."

The clip of Cas, with his arm around Chloe at the Bishop Frances reunion was shown over and over again. The off-color words at the microphone now seemed more outrageous than they did in the festive atmosphere of the reunion, and Cas appeared more wild eyed as his drunken rambling went on.

But Stacey also told the police that jealous girls at Chloe's school had been giving her a hard time both in person and online ever since she got the starring role on the *You've Got To Buy That Dress!* show. Chloe didn't want to go to school last week after someone anonymously posted a picture of her from the show with black eyes drawn on her face with "You've Got to Die in That Dress" written all over it. The principal sent a letter home that day warning students that threats will not be tolerated, and the school security guard promised to keep an extra eye on Chloe.

Chloe thought someone was following her when she walked to her classroom after the school day ended to get a book from her homeroom that she forgot to put in her backpack. When she turned around, her heart beating so fast she could not even breathe, the only person she saw was a maintenance man at the other end of the hall. She was too afraid to tell her mom, because she thought her mom would make her quit the show.

Stacey had been weirdly hesitant about Chloe appearing on the billboards and all over social media, and her reluctance made sense now. There were a lot of haters in the world, intent on bringing successful people down, and as Cas made it clear at the reunion, there were plenty of older men with a roving eye for the young ladies. Men who seemed charming and caring were certainly not all bad. There were some really great men in the world, and Stacey and Chloe knew some of the best. But many men were really bad; they took advantage of women with their comments, and worse, their actions.

Chapter 47

Chloe was cold, hungry, and most of all, terrified. Hours went by before she heard the door to the warehouse open again. Her heart was beating wildly, and she could see the tall, thin man, who was strangely familiar moving toward her. He loosed her hands and gave her a bag of fast food. She opened it and ate everything in the bag, feeling ravenous. She realized she had eaten nothing that day, anticipating that there would be a huge buffet of delicious food on the set as usual.

When she finished he bounded her hands again and chained her to the chair, this time pulling harder than he had before. She was sobbing when she managed to ask, "What are you going to do with me? I'm so scared, please don't hurt me."

Cas did not respond and instead simply turned around and left the building. It was cold in the room where she sat, and her feelings of despair deepened. She thought it must be getting dark outside and she just wanted to be home with her mom, dad and brother. Her eyes were adjusting to the dark, and she could see the large warehouse was mostly empty. She spotted her pink and white duffle bag and her brown leather backpack across the room in a corner. She wanted a blanket, or at least a scarf, something to keep her warm.

She started weeping. No one could hear her. What a difference one day makes. Yesterday she was over the moon with the expectation of everything the world had to offer. Today she was hoping merely to survive this ordeal and go home and be a typical teenager.

Back in Philadelphia, Nick Delmar was reviewing the blood work reports from the doctor Denise Ferraro visited just a couple of weeks before she died, when he noticed something he should double check. Though she had been ill, and exhibited all the signs of poisoning, her blood work came back normal. The report in Nick's hands was for a Denise Ferrara, and Nick wondered if it was just a typo, or a file mix-up.

He didn't want to discuss this over the phone, so he immediately drove to the hospital to share his concern with the records coordinator. In the meantime, hundreds of New York police officers searched for Chloe Gutton, last seen in brown boots, blue jeans, a pink tee shirt, a white puffer coat, and carrying a pink-striped duffel bag, and a brown leather backpack.

Scent dogs descended upon the area within a five mile radius of Port Authority, and Cas Ferraro's cell phone was being traced. The dogs were leading detectives toward Brooklyn, but there was no trace of Cas's phone.

When Nick got to the hospital, the records coordinator said that it appeared that Denise Ferraro's blood tests were confused with another patient, Denise Ferrara's blood work. Both women, coincidentally, had blood work done within a couple of weeks of one another. Denise Ferrara was re-tested for possible traces of mono ethylene glycol, or antifreeze. Denise Ferraro was said to be acting intoxicated and giddy in the weeks prior to her death, two symptoms often associated with sweet tasting ethylene glycol poisoning.

When Denise Ferrara was re-tested for poisoning, her blood came out clean because it was always clean. It was

Denise Ferraro who was dying of poisoning, undetected because the records mix-up.

Nick raced to call and tell Stacey, who had now been joined by Grant, Martin, Lisa, Nancy, and Zach. Eric came in and he and Martin jumped into Eric's unmarked car to begin searching.

There was an all-out manhunt for Cas Ferraro, in New York City, Philadelphia and Allentown, and Nick Delmar had an idea. He phoned his Uncle Walt for advice and then revealed his plan to get Chloe home safely. Cas was the number one suspect, and if anyone could get to him, it would be Stacey. Uncle Walt always believed that there is good and bad in everyone, even the most diabolical killer, and if you could appeal to their good side, in times of complete crisis and chaos, a good outcome was possible.

The evidence was mounting that Cas Ferraro poisoned his dead wife, and Chloe Gutton was likely in his clutches. This was a dangerous man, and they had to move fast.

Chapter 48

As instructed, Stacey texted Cas, "Hi Cas, I was hoping we could have a drink tonight," she tapped into her phone.

There was no response. She tried again.

"I'm free tonight, and I was hoping we could connect."

Her phone lit up.

"Oh, you want to see me now, do you?" he typed. Cas seemed angry and vindictive.

Stacey's hand was shaking as she typed in "Yes, of course I do," as instructed.

Cas very much wanted to see Stacey, but he wasn't stupid. When he left Chloe in the warehouse, he checked into a hotel under an assumed name, and turned on the TV. His photo and the video from the Bishop Frances reunion were everywhere.

This is why he installed an anti-trace device on his phone. There would be no way that the police could track him down, no matter how much he used his phone. He was able to scramble the cell tower reception so that his phone would ping from a tower miles away from where he actually was. He gave his lustrous hair a buzz cut, put on a battered, old Penn State baseball hat, added a mustache and an old jogging suit on with battered sneakers. He looked like a completely different person. Dapper Dan Cas Ferraro would not be caught dead dressed like this. He parked his car a mile from the hotel, walked in, and checked in under the name Fred Klein. There would be no way to find him.

The police told Stacey to be persistent. If she could wear down Cas's resolve and get to him, he might break and meet with her.

She pressed further. "May I speak to you, Cas? I miss you," she lied as she texted.

Cas loved her so deeply, but he was angry with her. How dare she rebuff Cas Ferraro.

You were nothing when you met me. I'm the big city IT guy. What are you really? Just a little, aging, first-generation business owner with 15 minutes of television fame? But at least I have Chloe, and Chloe looks just like you.

The police were divided on whether Stacey should bring up Chloe to Cas. They knew that they were dealing with a deranged person, and setting him off is the last thing that anyone wanted. Grant was holding Stacey up. She seemed to be one breath away from fainting. Here is a woman who did almost everything right: married a good man, built a respectable business, raised compassionate and bright children, sacrificed things for them, she was active in the community, she was a good sister and now, one wrong move and she has jeopardized all of it. She felt sick. She put her own child, her precious Chloe, in real danger. Stacey slumped to the floor.

I can't breathe.

Grant held Stacey in his arms, and she drew strength from his kindness and compassion.

"It's okay, Stacey, Chloe is going to be okay," he heard himself saying, but he didn't know if he could believe it. Their precious, only daughter was in real danger, and as a father, he felt that he had let it happen. Just as she was told to do, Stacey dialed Cas's phone, and he picked up.

"Cas, please, I want to see you," she lied. "I need you to help me find Chloe, she's missing," she added. Chief

Armstrong long believed that with kidnapping cases, the kidnapper wanted to be part of the solution. It was a strange psychological phenomenon. While he was solely responsible for endangering Chloe's life, police needed to make him think that he could help rescue Chloe by bringing her home safely.

"Why should I help you, Stacey?" Cas asked. "What will you do for me?"

"Cas, you know how I feel about you," Stacey said. Nick Delmar was convinced that if Stacey appealed to his love of her, Cas would crack, but they had to go in slowly. Cas hung up the phone and began walking toward the warehouse where Chloe was sitting, sobbing, in shock, desperate, cold and terrified. Cas pulled a burner phone from his pocket.

Just in case.

He dialed Stacey's number.

"Tell me how you feel about me," he pleaded. "Do you love me, Stacey?"

Stacey knew what she had to do. "Yes, Cas, of course," she said.

"Will you come to me? Forever?" he sounded increasingly unhinged.

"Yes, yes, Cas, where are you?" she asked.

"If you dare bring the police, you will never see your daughter again," he added.

By this time Martin and Eric were on the website for the geotracking company that Martin featured in his magazine years earlier. He had received dozens of little geotrackers as thank you gifts and remembered tucking one into Chloe's birthday bag from "Uncle Martin."

Martin told Stacey it was something for Chloe to keep in her backpack at all times and he was hoping that the little bag of beauty essentials might still be in Chloe's backpack. He knew she took her backpack everywhere, and it was confirmed that she had it went she disappeared. She never really cleaned it out. Miraculously, the geomap was showing that a geotracker was lighting up in Brooklyn. Could this lead them to Chloe? Neither man wanted to be too hopeful, but they had to move in the direction of the tracker, and every second counted. The website started circling down to the exact location. By this time, Martin and Eric were just fifteen minutes from Brooklyn.

The geotracker was taking them down a deserted street with wood pallets and chain linked fenced off warehouses. This was not the gentrified part of Brooklyn, this place was a dump. Suddenly, the geotracking started to beep, signaling that they were right on top of it, but all that Martin and Eric could see is a ramshackle old building with a large, rusted metal door.

"Chloe might be in there," Eric said. "Martin, wait here," he added, but Martin would have none of that.

Martin had been an Eagle Scout and a pilot, and he didn't want to wait in the car. He loved Chloe like a niece, and he wanted to be right there for her. Just seeing him would make Chloe believe that everything is all right.

Martin could not look more out of place in this run down back alley in Brooklyn if he tried. Dressed to the nines for a day at the salon, he had his grey, glen plaid double breasted Wren suit on and black Bruno Magli oxfords. Most men his age could never get away with the double breasted look, but his weight hadn't changed since high school and he looked just like he stepped out of *GQ*. For that reason, Eric asked him to stay in the car. After all, this was Eric's line of work. As a cop in Allentown, he dealt with drug dealers, even homicides, and had safely resolved dozens of domestic situations in the city. Admittedly, this was a beyond his usual "day in the squad car." Eric made sure his gun was loaded as he stepped out of the unmarked police car and began to walk toward the metal door to the warehouse as Martin stayed back. Eric convinced Martin that as a lookout he was providing an important service.

Chapter 49

In the meantime, Stacey was still keeping Cas on the phone in an effort to appeal to him to tell her where he had Chloe. Stacey was saying just what Nick had urged her to: "I love you, Cas, and I want to see you again."

She could barely say the words and not feel sick, but she was trying to do whatever she had to so that Chloe would be safe.

"I love you, too, Stacey," Cas said, and she could feel him softening. "Meet me on Fulton Street in Brooklyn. There's a bar and pizza place there called Juliana's. When can you be there?"

Stacey had already started making her way to New York with Grant, Nick, and Walt in the car. They were coming up to the Brooklyn Bridge when Cas asked to meet her. "I could be there in a few minutes," Stacey said.

"No cops," Cas said. "I'm warning you. Come alone. I want to see you," he added. Stacey's heart was beating out of her chest. She could hear helicopters searching for Chloe. Cas changed his direction to head toward Juliana's Pizza on foot. His large strides made the five minute walk even shorter.

In the meantime, Eric was making his way into the warehouse, and instead of acting as a lookout, Martin was just a few steps behind him. He knew that if Chloe was in there, she would not know she was safe if she saw "Uncle Martin." She didn't know Eric at all.

Chloe could hear the door to the warehouse open. Her

body, now in pain from the ties on her wrists, the cold and the sheer agony of the experience, braced for something ominous. Had he come back to her hurt. She had no idea what she would face. *I want my mommy. I want to go home.* Through the darkness she could see two men.

"Chloe?" Martin called out.

"Uncle Martin!?" Chloe started crying as she strained her eyes to see in the pitch darkness. Eric raced over to her and flashed his light on her. She looked okay. He cut the chains from her hands, and Martin swooped her up in his arms. As he was carrying her out the door, an almost unrecognizable Cas Ferraro was waiting for them.

"Where do you think you are going?" he asked Eric and Martin like a crazy man. Cas must have known it was over, but he acted otherwise, wielding a large knife. Just then, his phone rang and it was Stacey.

"Cas, I'm waiting for you," she said.

Enraged, Cas blurted out "Liar! You bitch! I killed my wife for you!" He tried to run, but by that time the entire warehouse was surrounded with the New York City police.

But it was Philadelphia officer Nick Delmar who read Cas Ferraro his rights while his Uncle Walt watched, beaming with pride. Chloe ran to Stacey and Grant for a large group hug. "

Are you okay, Chloe?" Stacey asked, horrified at what her precious daughter had to endure. She felt guilt like she had never felt in her life, but also gratitude. She resolved to never put her family in danger again, and to get help for her eating disorder. She needed to make peace with her parents deaths, take care of herself and her family and make the most of the life she had now, and the people who loved her.

Chapter 50

Brittany and Emily Ferraro were not one bit surprised to see their father in handcuffs and charged with the murder of their mother. They could never prove it themselves, but in their hearts they knew that their mother would never leave them. Nick Delmar brought all four Ferraro children together to give them the sad news. The youngest, Renee, took it the hardest. She was only 13 when her mother died, and could never fathom the incomprehensible thought that her father could be responsible for it. Cas, for all his failings and his sinister deeds, was also a decent father to his children. His son Clark hung his head in total despair when Nick told them their dad was arraigned and would be facing a trial if a plea deal was not made. There would be a good chance that their father would be behind bars for the rest of his life. There would be no more Ritz Carlton dinners or fancy suits for Cas Ferraro.

Denise's parents hugged Nick Delmar tight, the gratitude in their eyes palpable.

"We don't even know what to say," Gene said. Ann Wasnitsky handed Nick a medallion from Denise's candy striper uniform from her days as a volunteer at the hospital. It read: "To serve is to live."

"I want you to have this," Ann said. "Denise always wanted to serve others, and you have brought her spirit back to us with your selfless service in this case. We could never thank you. Denise is not coming back, we know that, but maybe now she could rest in peace."

Nick wiped tears from his eyes, and thought about how Uncle Walt always told him that it wasn't the paycheck that made the job worthwhile—it was the impact on people's lives. This was what he meant. And it meant so much to come through for Uncle Walt. This is the one case that bothered him. He knew that something just was not right. Nick could only hope that he had half of Uncle Walt's instincts in the future.

Chapter 51

Chloe embraced her Uncle Martin as if she would never let him go.

"Glad I popped one of those geo trackers in your birthday bag, kiddo," he said. "If I hadn't introduced myself to the owner of the company, he never would have given them to me."

"Oh, Uncle Martin, you are my hero," Chloe said.

Uncle Martin said, "Remember, it's not who you know,"

Chloe finished, "It's who you let know you!"

Martin felt especially pleased with himself because he knew that he had played a significant role in finding Chloe. Without him, it isn't certain whether she would have made it home safely.

Stacey embraced Martin with everything she had and said, "Martin, you are my chosen family. I love you, and I don't think I can ever repay you for this."

When they finally made their way home that night, Stacey, Grant, Chloe and Zach each felt like they belonged to the best and luckiest family in the world. Suddenly Stacey didn't care that they had a rather odd, overbuilt country home in the middle of nowhere. Home, however flawed it might have looked to her before, now seemed quite perfect. Grant turned up the heat and let the outdoor lights on overnight. Zach stopped teasing Chloe about algebra, and took the garbage out without even being told. Chloe promised to never miss another day of high school and to work extra hard on her college essays and exams. So keyed up from the day's traumatic events, Stacey was wide-eyed well past midnight. Grant turned to her, put his arm around her and smiled softly, saying, "I love you, Stacey, I am here to really listen to you, and everything will be alright."

It was true, Stacey thought, that no one was all good or all bad, and she was eternally grateful that nothing so bad happened to all this good in her life. And the best part of her life, her loving family, was right in front of her.

Chapter 52

Casimir Ferraro was found guilty of murder by poisoning of his wife Denise Wasnitsky Ferraro, and was also convicted of stalking and kidnapping with the intent to harm. With his head hung in despair, he was sentenced to life in prison without the possibility of parole. He would be trading in his cuff links for handcuffs, and his sad grey eyes blended in with the washed out charcoal colored prison issued pants and shirt.

The Ferraro children, though terribly sad about both of their parents' fates, were taken care of by Denise's parents. Their mother's life insurance secured their financial future. The memory of Denise Wasnitsky was preserved by her four loving children who sponsored a mental health awareness week every year at the hospital where Brittany worked. It was their goal to help other families dealing with mental illness seek support. Neighbors from their old community came to celebrate the loving mother. All four children, and their grandparents formed a loving, close-knit bond.

Chapter 53

Stacey certainly did not have any insight into her constant, burning question about why some people live and others die, but now she finally realized that she may never have answers. She still missed her parents, but she knew that living each day as though it was her last would be the best way to honor them and the fragility of life.

Still a fervent reader of the obituaries, but less obsessed with her own legacy, Stacey felt content to have quiet, constant and positive impact on the lives of her own family, instead of seeking any kind of confirmation from the outside world of her worth and value. She knew for sure that everyone could be both good and bad in different ways. She was positive that while everyone is traceable in some way, knowing where her loved ones stood with her would be all the geotracking she needed.

Working to have more honest relationships with everyone in her life made Stacey seek the help she needed to stop chewing and spitting, a highly dangerous, addictive eating disorder. And though she had hoped her obituary was nowhere near ready for publication, she was actually starting to like the way that her life story would someday read.

It was late Sunday morning, and Stacey put her newspaper down and turned her phone off for the rest of the day. She and Grant looked at each other with the warmth and love of an old married couple, and yet with the frisson of a fresh start.

Book Club Guide Questions:

1. Even though it is quite understandable that Stacey still misses her parents, more than a decade after their deaths, do you think her grief is lasting longer than most grown children's grief for their lost parents?
2. Stacey often reflects that "blood is thicker than water." What does that mean and do you agree?
3. Do you think that Stacey treats Grant with respect? What advice would you give them for their marriage to be stronger?
4. Why do you think Grant is so obsessed with saving money, to the point of discomfort to his family?
5. What role do Betta and Isaac play in the lives of Grant and Stacey?
6. Why does Stacey find obituaries so fascinating?
7. Is Stacey's obsession with staying under 135 pounds odd?
8. Is chewing and spitting a dangerous eating disorder?
9. Had you heard about it before you read this book?
10. Is Cas good or bad? What are your thoughts about people being all good or all bad?
11. What did Stacey realize about the impact of her life?

Useful Websites

www.nami.org

www.nationaleatingdisorders.org

www.nationaleatingdisorders.org/blog/5-things-you-didn%E2%80%99t-know-about-chewing-and-spitting-disorder

www.verwellmind.com

www.verywellmind.com/chew-and-spit-eating-disorder-behavior-4100664

www.Womenshealthmag.com

www.womenshealthmag.com/health/eating-disorder-chew-and-spit

JUST LIKE YOU is a work of fiction. But like Nora Ephron famously said, "everything is copy." Names, characters, businesses, places, events, locales, and incidents are used in a fictitious manner. I may have drawn upon people I have known or know, but any true resemblance to actual persons, living or dead, or actual events is either coincidental or meant as a fond tribute to characteristics so memorable that they deserve to be immortalized. You know who you are.

Acknowledgements: First and foremost: thank you to my family for love and life. There is no doubt in my mind who you really are. Special thanks to Penny Eifrig and Eifrig Publishing and Mt. Nittany Press for her support and dedication to amplify voices often left unheard, and to Ken Womack for his sage advice, positivity and guidance as I leapt into the world of fiction writing. A special thanks to Abby Kennedy for painstakingly copyediting this book toward the end of a busy master's degree and year of teaching.

About the Author: Nichola D. Gutgold is a professor of communication arts and sciences for Penn State Lehigh Valley who researches women in non-traditional fields. She has written numerous books on women in non-traditional fields. This is her first book of fiction.

Made in the USA
Middletown, DE
22 May 2018